D1002168

HELL'S CAÑON

Other Five Star Titles
by T. T. Flynn:

Night of the Comanche Moon (1995)
Rawhide (1996)
Long Journey to Deep Cañon (1997)
Death Marks Time in Trampas (1998)
The Devil's Lode (1999)
Ride to Glory (2000)
Prodigal of Death (2001)

HELL'S CAÑON

A Western Quintet

T. T. FLYNN

Five Star • Waterville, Maine

Five Star First Edition Western Series.

Published in 2002 in conjunction with Golden West Literary Agency.

Cover design by Thorndike Press Staff.

Set in 11 pt. Plantin.

Printed in the United States on permanent paper.

Library of Congress Cataloging-in-Publication Data

Flynn, T. T.
Hell's cañon : a Western quintet / by T. T. Flynn.
p. cm.
ISBN 0-7862-3541-1 (hc : alk. paper)
1. Western stories.
PS3556.L93 H45 2002
813′.54—dc21 2002020558

Table of Contents

Satan's Deputy

T. T. Flynn completed "Satan's Deputy" on September 6, 1933. It was the sixteenth story he had written that year, and it was accepted immediately upon arrival by *Star Western*, published by Popular Publications. The first issue of *Star Western*, published in October, 1933, had had as its lead story Flynn's "Hell's Half-Acre," a story he originally titled "Conquistador's Gold" and which has been collected under his original title in *Rawhide: A Western Quintet* (Five Star Westerns, 1966), now also available in a paperback edition published by Leisure Books. Flynn wasn't in the second issue of this monthly magazine, but with "Satan's Deputy" he was headlined on the cover of the third issue, dated December, 1933. He was paid $365.00 by the magazine for this story upon acceptance.

I

"EXODUS"

Pallor lay gray-white on Sundown Daly's face as he stepped into the warden's office—prison pallor. They had prisons in the cow country in those days. The lack of sunlight and fresh air that had caused the pallor had not touched the man beneath. Sundown Daly's shoulders were as broad and massive as the day he had entered the barred prison gates two years before. He was thinner, leaner, harder. Corded muscles stood out under his rough prison shirt, and his hands were callused with toil. One thing about him was new; one thing prison had stamped deep: cold bitterness—etched in the lines of his face, burning deeply in his steady gaze.

The warden's office was high-ceilinged, filled with heavy black hardwood furniture. The windows were high and narrow. Not much light came through them. It was a shadowy office, heavy with rigid rules, lost liberty, little different from the gray stone cell-blocks where men smoldered in sullen resentment.

Two other men were in the office. Before the roll-top desk sat Warden Bursey—short, pompous, pudgy, an irascible political cipher who had been placed over helpless men, for better or worse. The second man, slouched low in a chair beside the window, was long and broad-shouldered, with iron-gray hair. His face, behind a black mustache, was lean, hard, and deeply tanned by sun and wind. A pair of worn riding boots reached up inside his trousers. A cartridge belt and holster were slung under his coat. A dusty Stetson was tossed on a chair nearby.

All that Sundown Daly saw with one quick glance. Then his eyes went past the warden, past the seated man, out the window to the sunlight and open range.

The warden wheeled in his chair and stood up. "So, it's you, Daly. You're going out in five minutes. Twelve o'clock, noon." He glanced at the wooden clock ticking on the wall above his desk and repeated: "In five minutes."

Daly pulled his eyes away from the scene beyond the window. His glance smoldered as it rested on the warden. "You don't have to tell me," he said without emotion. "I've had the day an' hour marked for two years."

The warden's plump cheeks reddened. "No back talk!" he

snapped. "You're still a prisoner!"

Daly looked down at the warden, and a thin smile of contempt came over his face. "I can wait five minutes," he said softly.

The warden's plump fingers flicked the edge of his desk angrily. "You prisoners all assert your liberty as soon as possible! But I won't have it in here! Understand?"

"I hear you." Daly yawned.

The warden scowled helplessly, reddened. "There are a few details!" he snapped. "The state allows you mileage to the town from which you were sentenced. And we are holding some money for you."

"Three hundred an' seventy-five dollars . . . and six bits." Daly nodded.

The warden opened a drawer and laid a brown manila envelope on the desk. "It's in here, with stage fare to Las Piedras, where you were committed."

Daly took the envelope, scanned the contents briefly, thrust it in a pocket of his ill-fitting prison suit. "Anything more?" he asked slowly.

"Yes. It is my duty as warden to give you a few words of advice."

Daly shrugged. "Spare your advice, Warden. I've listened to you bleat and whinny before. Your little lecture makes most of the boys laugh. It'd only spoil the taste of the ham an' eggs I'm gonna buy."

The tall stranger, lounging by the window, pushed back his coat and brought out tobacco and papers. He had been watching the interchange. A sheriff's badge, pinned inside his coat, showed briefly, but the prisoner did not see it.

The warden was almost apoplectic. "Damn your impudence! I wish it were possible to put you on bread and water for that! I merely wanted to warn you that you have paid your debt to society. From now on the rest is up to you. We don't want to see you in here again."

Daly's gaze wandered out the window again, then came back to the warden, steady and cold. "I reckon you'd like to have me back in your private hell hole, Warden. It'd do that mean little soul of yours good to see me bulldogged an' hog-tied again. But you won't. This society you bleat about is only crooked law. I wasn't wanted on Las Piedras range, so they hustled me off. Dealt me jokers an' aces an' called the play. Now *I'm* dealin, Warden." Daly leaned forward. His voice rang bitterly, terrible in the quiet of the room. *"They made me an outlaw . . . and I'm staying one! Savvy?"*

"You're talking like a fool, Daly."

Daly doubled his great hands into great fists, flexed his arms so that the mighty muscles writhed and crawled under his shirt. He laughed at the warden again. It was not a nice thing to hear, that laugh.

"Don't cross my gunsight, Warden. An' to give that crawling little mind of yours something to think about, I'm riding to the Red McKays in the mountains east of Las Piedras. Throw that in the teeth of this society you're representin' without much credit."

"The Red McKays!" exclaimed the warden angrily. "Then I'll have the pleasure of hanging you before long, Daly. Wallace, you heard this man!"

The big gray-haired figure in the chair nodded slowly, inhaling deeply from his cigarette and seeping smoke slowly through his mustache. His eyes roved over the prisoner appraisingly.

"Daly," he said calmly, "if you join the Red McKays, you'll get shot or hung sooner or later. I'm the new sheriff up that way. And I'm going to clean out that nest of buzzards before I leave office."

Daly's gaze narrowed as he studied Wallace. There was no fear or surprise in his manner, rather cool estimation, as if weighing a man he would one day meet.

"Much obliged for the warning," he said laconically. "Come with your guns out when you start after me."

"I'll be lookin' for you when I get back, Daly."

"I'll be there."

The wooden clock on the wall slowly chimed twelve strokes. Daly's great chest swelled as he breathed deeply. His shoulders went back.

"That lets me out, Warden. An' I'll see you in hell on judgment day. Bad luck to you till then."

Daly swung on his heel and strode out of the dingy office. The warden choked out an oath as the door closed.

II

"FOOD FOR THE GALLOWS"

It was late afternoon when the big black splashed across the sandy shallows and muddy trickle that was the Río Osito —Little Bear River. The low sun was still hot. Spurts of dust drifted up behind the black's hoofs as he climbed the rise beyond the river.

The country around was rolling, broken, gaunt bare breaks and flat-topped mesas, pebbly red soil, barren and dry. Scant bunch grass, rabbit weed, and greasewood struggled to live in that dry soil, and now and then stunted cholla cactus and scanty prickly pear showed defiant spines.

It was a dry world, a harsh, lonely, desolate world—to the casual eye. No houses, no cattle, no life, save one lone hawk sailing low on motionless pinions, fiercely scanning the ground for unwary rodents. But to the impassive rider on the big black it was not lonely, desolate, or harsh. This was everything he had waited for, lived for. Two days of sun had already struck hard at the prison pallor. Sundown Daly's great shoulders were squarer, his movements freer, his glance quick and alert.

The black shied suddenly. A dry warning rattle broke out on the ground. With a single effortless sweep Daly plucked the revolver from his right leg and fired. As the black cantered on, dark coils thrashed and flowed helplessly on the reddish ground.

Daly laughed aloud with satisfaction as he holstered the .45 and reached to the spotted-hair vest for makings. "If that had been a man, he'd've stayed there," he said aloud.

A new person rolled that smoke deftly, and flipped the match away, a changed person from the ill-dressed prisoner who had thrown defiance in the warden's teeth. A black sombrero, already well-powdered with dust, sat jauntily on Sundown Daly's head. A scarlet handkerchief hung about his neck. Fancy-stitched half boots and gay silver spurs were on his feet. A rifle was thrust into a leather saddle boot. Two guns swung at his hips. Behind him a saddle roll was lashed, with coat and slicker on top. All new—bought in those first few hours of freedom.

He was a lean, hard, eager man, this Sundown Daly, who journeyed toward those distant mountains with a cold, fixed purpose. Hughie Jennings had given him the key to the Red McKays—Hughie Jennings, who had ridden with the McKays and was now doing life inside the high brick walls of the prison.

A rash man would have ridden straight to Las Piedras. Two years had taught Daly caution. They would be expecting him at Las Piedras. If they had framed him once, they could again. Las Piedras could wait.

The sun dropped low to the western skyline. The heat began to fade. There was a road somewhere ahead, leading to a rude collection of adobe huts called Paradise. Daly knew its two saloons and one general store that served the ranch country hereabouts. A drink at one of the bars, a few needed purchases, and he'd push on and sleep out.

So he rode steadily, and the sun sank from sight. Heavy purple twilight came rolling out of the east. The swift chill of night dropped down. But there was light enough to show the cloud of dust moving along the road ahead. Daly marked it, ignored it. His mind was on other things when he rode around a tumbled mass of eroded rock and the winding road confronted him a few yards below.

A quick pull on the reins stopped the horse. The stage that had raised the dust stood there in the road. The four horses were still blowing hard from their run, champing bits, throwing their heads. And something was wrong. Very wrong!

Four, no, five men were lined up beside the stage. A lone rider on a short-coupled roan confronted them. Daly hardly needed the glimpse of a red bandanna mask and drawn revolver to get the truth. His first instinctive move brought a gun into his hand. Then he remembered this was none of his business.

The passengers, lined up beside the stage, stared at him. The masked rider shot a quick, oblique look. Just an instant he was off guard. In the dim light a man's hand snapped down to his vest. A tiny Derringer barked as the masked rider looked back.

The shot struck squarely. The bandit swayed in the saddle.

"Got him," Daly muttered. "Good shot!"

A second spat of the Derringer was drowned in the louder roar of a belt gun. The rash passenger fell back against the rear wheel, crumpling to the ground. The others were already scattering out of range. The masked rider fired twice after them—high, evidently, as no one dropped. Then he reined his horse behind the stage, spurred off beyond the road. Daly saw that he gripped the saddle horn with one steadying hand as he went.

Daly rode down to the stage, holstering his gun. The rash owner of the Derringer lay crumpled and still in the dust.

"Hey! Come back!" Daly called to the passengers.

His answer was a gunshot over a large rock ahead of the stage. The bullet whined viciously past his head. Daly ducked, shouted: "You damn' fool! Stop that! I ain't. . . ."

A second shot cut off his words. Splinters flew as lead raked the edge of the open stage door. Another gun behind another rock barked out. The bullet tore through the high crown of Daly's sombrero. Too close for comfort. He reined about and spurred for safety, using the stage for cover.

The light was poor, the men excited. They threw shots after him—and all missed. He made the first curve safely, and without warning found himself riding directly into a bunch of horsemen racing up the road toward the stage.

They were all about him an instant later. Six of them—cowmen by their looks—and none too friendly. A chunky man in overalls reined in close, resting a big Colt across his saddle horn.

"What's all the shootin' about, stranger?" he demanded truculently. "How come you're hightailin' down the road thisaway?"

Daly grinned at them. "Running to keep my hair," he said coolly. He removed his sombrero, poked a finger through the bullet hole in the crown. "Stage was held up," he explained.

"I came along an' got mistook for the rannihan who did it! They opened up on me, an' I left."

"Mistook, eh? Ride back with us, stranger, an' we'll see. We thought somebody had took a crack at that stage when we heard the shootin'." It was the chunky man with the gun speaking, and his manner brooked little argument.

Daly had none to give. "Let's go." He nodded.

The stage passengers were gathering by the prone figure in the dust when they rode up. A tall, lanky man with a shotgun in one hand stared at them, and then called out: "Why'n hell didn't you boys get here sooner? I knowed you was behind us an' was hopin'. Might have saved Weber's life."

The chunky one beside Daly exclaimed: "That Dan Weber on the ground?"

"Uhn-huh. Drilled through the neck."

"Who done it? This feller?"

The man with the shotgun looked hard in the gathering darkness, and then shook his head. "Nope. His pardner done it. This 'un stayed hid up there by the rocks an' held a gun on us."

"You're loco, stranger!" Daly snapped. "I didn't know it was a hold-up till I rode around them rocks. I never laid eyes on that curly wolf before."

"Lyin' won't help you any!" was the curt answer he got. "We all seen you over there holdin' a gun on us. An' didn't you hightail down the road?"

"You'd've left twice as fast if you'd been on my end of all that shootin'," Daly retorted.

The man with the shotgun spat on the ground. "You've had time to think of a good story, mister. But it won't go. Chuck, you an' the boys better bring him into Paradise. There's a deputy there can take him for murder . . . if the boys don't lynch 'im first. Dan Weber was well thought of around here."

"Sure, we'll do that," the chunky one growled, and said to Daly: "Gimme your guns, an' ride peaceable or we'll save the law trouble!"

In the black dusk Sundown Daly's mouth twisted in bitter humor. Two years in prison—two days out, and back for murder. He wouldn't have a chance. His record, his statement to Warden Bursey, would give the lie to any defense.

"Gimme your guns!" the chunky one demanded again roughly. He leaned over to empty the nearest holster.

Daly caught his wrist, yanked hard.

The chunky one yelled—"Get him, boys!"—as he toppled from the saddle and grabbed leather.

Raking spurs sent Daly's horse lunging into the next animal, driving it reeling. They caromed into a third horse, burst through the circle of riders, and bolted past the rear of the stage.

It was sudden, unexpected. The men were jammed in too close for wild gunfire. Once more the stage screened Daly for a few seconds while he left the road and spurred up the bank beyond. Gathering dusk closed in behind him as a fusillade of shots erupted on the road. He fired back twice as the drumming hoofs of the big horse carried him over the low hogback and out of sight.

They followed. Stray shots at first, searching the night, then the steady pounding of hoofs. But darkness came fast, and there was no moon.

Daly plunged down a steep arroyo bank and pounded along the twisting sandy channel. When he reined up and listened, the night lay, silent and heavy, about him. The pursuit had blundered off in some other direction.

He rode another half mile in the arroyo, and then turned out and headed west, away from the road, away from Paradise and the route he had been following.

An all-night ride lay ahead if the horse could stand it. A posse would probably be on the trail before long. Daly smiled wryly as he settled himself in the saddle and faced the night.

"Two days out of that stone corral and they're ready to stretch the Daly neck," he said aloud. "The warden must've had a vision when he warned me."

The black nickered as he trotted easily through the darkness, sure-footed, willing. But a little later, when skirting a patch of brush, he shied, snorted.

Nearby another horse snorted, stamped uneasily. Daly's gun leaped into his hand. Dimly he could see the shadowy bulk of the other horse.

"Speak up!" he warned the darkness sharply.

Two long seconds passed without an answer—and then a gasp came from the ground beside the shadowy horse.

"I got you covered!" a voice choked. "Keep ridin' or I'll drill you!" A strangling cough was followed by harsh, labored breathing.

Daly could just see the darker splotch of a form on the ground. Slowly he holstered his gun.

"You've got lead in your chest," he guessed shrewdly.

The strangling cough broke out again. The man on the ground cleared his throat with difficulty. "I ain't answerin' questions, or askin' none. Head off from here an' travel fast."

"You're the rannihan who held up the stage," Daly guessed coolly. "I seen that feller plugged you with his Derringer. You couldn't make it beyond here so you fell off to sit it out."

A bitter oath was an answer. "I've still got a gun!" the labored voice threatened from the ground. "Ride on before I make it two I've plugged!"

"Sure, sure," Daly agreed hastily. "Calm down. That won't help you none. They're ridin' this way. They'll cut your trail or mine sooner or later."

"What's your trail got to do with it?"

"I'm the *hombre* who busted in on your little play," Daly said brusquely. "They opened up on me after you left, and ran me down the road into a bunch of waddies smoking along to see what the excitement was. It seems I was helping you, and they figgered a bird in the pot was worth two out in the brush, so they elected me to hang for you. I never did like to hang, so I lit out. And now, stranger, you'd better drop that gun, if you've still got strength to raise it. You made me an outlaw back there. Some *hombre* said there's honor among thieves, so we might as well talk it over!" Daly swung to the ground.

"You know too damn much to be makin' it up," the stranger admitted with an effort. "But if you're fixin' to double deal me, I'll plug you yet."

"You wrong me, stranger," Daly said ironically. "Where'd he hit you?"

"In the chest."

The stranger was lying there on the ground, the reins hooked around an arm. He moved slightly as Daly squatted beside him. The faint *click* of a trigger cocking nicked the night sharply.

"Hold on," Daly warned calmly. "I'm gonna scratch a match so we can get better acquainted."

He flicked the match head with a thumbnail, cupping the flame cautiously in his hands. In the faint yellow glow a young face, tortured, white, sprang out at him. Crimson stained the mouth corners. The sunken eyes were bright with fever, suffering.

Even while the match flared, another choking cough racked the figure, so badly this time that the cocked revolver dropped on the ground and was forgotten. Flecks of bloody foam appeared. When the spasm was over, the youth—he was little more than that—laid limply, exhausted on the ground.

Daly flicked the charred end of the match and swore. "Hell . . . you're only a kid! And you're hit bad. I'll see what I can do about it."

"Save your trouble," was the muttered response. "A doctor couldn't help. It's in the chest, near the heart. Hole's closed up and bleedin' bad inside. I'm cashin' in, an' I know it!"

Daly recognized it for the truth. He rolled a cigarette in the darkness as he squatted silently.

"What's the name?" he queried with odd gentleness for the man the world knew as Sundown Daly. "I'm Daly, just out of two years in the pen, and headin' for a necktie party if the posse catches up with me."

With a panting effort the young man stirred and lifted his head. "Sundown Daly?" he husked.

"Uhn-huh. Don't say we've met."

"No, but I've heard about you," the boy muttered. "I remember when they tried you at Las Piedras. You shot a deputy."

"That's what they said," Daly agreed. "Found my gun by the water hole where it happened. An' next day I showed up with a bullet in my shoulder. I was lucky to get off with two years."

"I heard talk that maybe Yance Claggett knew more about that than you did."

"You hear talk," Daly agreed, but in the darkness his face went hard.

"I figgered that talk was right."

"Mebbe so," Daly grunted. "Let's forget about me and the Claggetts. What's your name? How come a bright young feller like you lined up a stage full of passengers and made gun talk? Just tired of working for forty a month?"

Another spasm of coughing—and the voice came, weaker this time. "Wanted money. Wanted to go home with my pockets full. My old man needs it bad."

Daly was noncommittal.

"I've heard Sundown Daly was a square shooter."

"I knew him when he was," Daly said briefly.

"Listen to me." A hand groped weakly to Daly's knee. "I ain't gonna leave here. What the posse'll find won't do 'em any good. This ain't any of your business . . . but a dyin' man rates a favor. Take that bag back of my saddle an' hand it to my sister. Tell her . . . anything . . . but leave the stage out. I ain't known around here. I reckon they won't take much trouble to find out who I am. Will you do that?"

Sundown Daly, whose hand was against every man's, who rode now toward the Red McKays, man-killers, rustlers, terrors of the high range east of the Las Piedras, found himself answering gruffly, lying earnestly: "I'll take it to her if you can't make it, but you'll pull out of this, son."

Another spasm of coughing shook the boy. "Nope!" he gasped. "No need to lie to me. My number's up. I'm slippin' fast. I can feel it."

Daly did not argue. The boy was right. And no man ever faced death more calmly. "What makes you so sure I'll do it?" Daly asked evenly.

"Sundown Daly would."

"Thanks," said Daly briefly. He inhaled, dribbled smoke through his nostrils. "Where does your sister live?" he asked abruptly. "What's her name?"

III

"NIGHT RIDERS"

The darkness hid the boy's sigh of relief. His voice was choked as he said: "You're white, Sundown Daly. Go to the Wagon Wheel Ranch an' ask for Jordan Lee."

Daylight would have shown startled surprise on Daly's face. The blackness hid it now. His voice came casual. "Wagon Wheel brand, eh? Seems to me I've heard of it. Feller by the name of Enoch Lee owned it."

"My father."

"Jordan Lee," Daly mused. "That's a purdy name, and a queer one. Never heard a girl called that before."

"The old man went to the Bible to name us. I'm Mark Lee. Ride up an' ask for Jordan. Give her my saddlebags. Tell her I always thought she was a pretty swell sister . . . even if I never said much about it." Mark Lee's voice ran off into a laboring whisper, lapsed into the silence.

The horses moved restlessly, shaking their heads now and then. Far off into the west the weird yapping of coyotes drifted through the night intermittently. It was dark here, lonely, and the cool breeze seemed chillier with the tragedy that was drawing in quickly and certainly.

Sundown finished his cigarette, rolled another, lit it. The match light showed young Mark Lee resting with his eyes closed, barely breathing. Sundown shook his head regretfully. The harsh lines in his face were softer. He was about to flip the second cigarette away when the distant, almost inaudible, pound of horses' hoofs drifted through the silence.

"They're coming!" Sundown said aloud.

No answer.

"You hear me, kid?"

Young Mark Lee was still, quiet. Sundown leaned forward, found a wrist that had no pulse in it. He got to his feet, drawing a deep breath. It was over. Mark Lee had gone, leaving the burden of his transgressions behind him for another man to face.

It was characteristic of Sundown Daly that he wasted no time. He searched the body for papers, found none. Swiftly he moved the saddlebags to his own horse. The riders were nearer now, probably searching blindly but nonetheless grimly in the darkness.

Sundown took the reins of Mark Lee's horse and swung up into his own saddle. Silently he rode away, leading the extra horse. It was well he did. The hard day's ride had weakened the black. It was not long before he began to tire. Sundown shifted to the other horse and rode on.

The gray false dawn found horses and man sodden with weariness. They were in the foothills now, treading through piñon and cedar that shut them in and barred out the world beyond. In the gray semidarkness of dawn they came to a narrow stream tumbling out of the higher hills.

Sundown let the horses drink sparingly, and then rode for some two miles up the winding, rocky watercourse. There he cut off to the left to higher ground. Some fifteen minutes later he paused in an open space at the crest of a hill. Beyond, other slopes rolled up and up into the scarlet and gold glory of sunrise. Below, the green, piñon-covered slopes over which he had come met the dry mesa that stretched as far as the eye could reach.

The panorama was stupendous, with hazy purple mountains rimming the far horizon. But Sundown's bloodshot eyes looked for other things than beauty. He saw no dust that marked riders, no moving dots that looked suspicious. With a grunt of relief he clambered out of the saddle, tied the two horses to a piñon tree, and dropped on the ground beside them. They would have to wait for food and water, staying close and secure where he could be in the saddle in a moment's notice.

Within two minutes he was sound asleep.

Sundown was up at high noon, grimy, unshaven, but refreshed. The horses drooped where he had tied them. Sunlight and shadows checker-boarded vividly back through the trees. Below, over the mesa country, the heat haze thickened into the far distance. Still there was no sign of pursuit.

Sundown stretched, yawned, tilted his black sombrero over his eyes to break the sun glare, and inspected the horses carefully. They were gaunted, worn, obviously needing rest, forage, water. But there was still hard riding left in their wiry muscles. Sundown mounted, took the reins of Mark Lee's horse, and rode off, whistling softly through his teeth.

All that afternoon he rode through the foothills, climbing the descending steep slopes. Always he made his trail among the piñons and tall cedars. When the sun dropped to the western horizon, and the shadows were long, and the night not far off, he angled down into the grass and easier going.

The country had changed about him. The grass was greener, taller. Small bunches of white faces were grazing here and there. In the far distance, another three hours' riding, was Las Piedras. Not far ahead was Cowpen Creek, and, if one followed the sprawling, sandy bed of Cowpen Creek, one came to the Wagon Wheel Ranch, to Jordan Lee who had been a fine sister. Sundown rode to Cowpen Creek.

The water was low, a mere trickle in the wide, sandy bed. The sand muffled his progress as he rode into the dusk. A little more and he'd be at the Wagon Wheel, his errand discharged, his way free into the hills.

Sundown's face went harder, his shoulders drew back as he thought of that. In the hills were freedom and men who laughed at the law that sought them. As he thought of that, he heard the low bawl of cattle nearby, and close on that the sharp explosion of a gun.

Sundown neck-reined the black over to the bank and up into the shelter of a juniper clump. Gunshots meant trouble.

Other shots, swift, staccato, venomous, burst through the dusk as he rode to shelter. There was no whine of lead. The shots were coming from across the stream, beyond the rise of the opposite bank. Rifle in hand, Sundown waited, searching that wooded rim with narrowed eyes.

Then, of a sudden, a horseman burst into view against the skyline. He was riding hard, leaning low in the saddle, slashing with the romal ends, spurring furiously. A sombrero fell from his head as he thundered down the slope toward the sandy creekbed. He ignored it. Sundown saw a belt gun glint in his hand, saw him throw one hasty glance over his shoulder, and then set himself as the horse plunged over a two-foot bank into the creekbed.

There were no more shots, but one knew instinctively that death was not far behind the fleeing man. Almost as suddenly as the first man had appeared, two more riders burst into view at the top of the slope. They reined sharply, their horses sliding to a halt. They carried rifles. They whipped them to their shoulders. Their drumming reports smote almost as one shot.

The horse shied, whirled off at a tangent. The rider toppled from the saddle, struck the damp sand full length. He rolled limply, gun flying from his hand, stopped on his face, shuddered, lay still. The horse bolted up the slope, reins flying loose, stirrups flapping.

The horse Sundown was leading shied, snorted. "Hold still!" Sundown said savagely, and yanked the rebellious animal in close.

But it was too late. He had been seen. Two rifles covered the spot. A voice shouted: "Ride out in the open and let's see you!"

"Not while you're droppin' men out of the saddle like that!" Sundown called back. "If you're aimin' to pop me, try it from there!"

It was a tense moment. The two men spoke to each other in low tones. They seemed undecided.

"If it's gun talk you want, open up. If it ain't, ride back, or come down to the water and meet me!" Sundown called to them.

"Hold it!" one of them shouted. "We're comin' down!"

Slowly, watchfully, they walked their horses down to the bed of Cowpen Creek, and Sundown rode equally as slowly and watchfully to meet them. Three rifles covered targets. Three fingers crooked tense for the first sign of treachery as they met by the limp form on the sand.

Sundown asked coolly: "What's all the excitement about?"

The man on the right was small, slender, stoop-shouldered, with a wizened, shrewd face, and a tangle of uncut hair showing beneath the brim of a worn, battered Stetson. He wore one gun and a belt knife. A manila lass rope was tied at his saddle horn. His cowhide chaps were as worn as his Stetson, and he sat silently, watchfully, as his companion answered: "We're dealin' questions here, stranger.

What's your handle an' your business? You ain't a Wagon Wheel man."

The speaker could have made two of his companion. He was a big man, lean and rangy, a young man, with a carefully trimmed red mustache, something of a dandy, too, in chaps decorated with silver *conchos*. His saddle was fine leather, his bridle studded with silver *conchos,* also. A silk handkerchief was tied about his neck. A big sombrero was cocked at a rakish angle. Two guns, slung low on his hips, had mother-of-pearl and silver inlaid in the handles.

His voice was harsh, commanding. He showed no regret or excitement at having killed a man. His eyes did not even drop to the body on the ground.

Sundown watched them both narrowly. He had a vague feeling that he should know them, but could not place the men. Sparring for time, he asked: "Is this Wagon Wheel range?"

He got a gruff reply: "I reckon you know where you are, stranger. Speak up while you got time! We're in a hurry!"

The little man watched Sundown intently. The round hole in the muzzle of his rifle was like an unwinking eye, threatening, vicious. The wizened face was a mask, a killer's mask.

Sundown weighed the odds swiftly. He might get one in a showdown. The other would probably finish him off. They were not men who bluffed. They had killed once and could easily do so again.

Sundown shrugged and dismissed the odds. His face was hard as he rasped: "They call me Sundown Daly. There's a posse lookin' for me. I'm just out of two years in the pen. This *hombre* you plugged is your business. We'll let the deal stay that way. If you don't like it, call your bet."

The two exchanged a quick glance. The tension visibly relaxed. The little man lowered his rifle, said softly: "I reckon it's him, Rex. Didn't Hughie Jennings write he shaped up about like this?"

Sundown placed them then. He smiled thinly and lowered his rifle, also. "You're Rex McKay," he said to the big dandy, "old Jupiter McKay's youngest. That mustache fooled me. Hughie Jennings said you were clean-faced."

The little man chortled dryly. "He's grown up."

That got him a scowl. "Shut up, Salty! Your humor gives me a pain in the neck."

"You'll be Salty O'Shea," Sundown said to the little man. "Hughie Jennings says you'd rather shoot a man than eat a sirloin."

Salty O'Shea grinned, in no wise offended.

Rex McKay was still suspicious. Rifle ready, he growled: "Where'd you meet Hughie Jennings?"

"In the pen. He's doing life, but figgers he'll be out before long."

"Where you headin'?"

"To your outfit. Any arguments?"

"Put up your gun," said Rex McKay. He slipped his own rifle in the saddle boot. Sundown followed suit. Salty O'Shea did the same. But Sundown noted that Rex McKay hooked a thumb in his belt within easy reach of pearl-mounted gun handles as he eyed him narrowly. "You're headin' away from the McKay range," he pointed out curtly. "How come?"

"Business at the Wagon Wheel ranch house, then I'm ridin' back in the hills."

"What's your business at the Wagon Wheel, Daly?"

"Private," Sundown said calmly. "Tend to your own business an' don't pry in mine. It ain't done in polite society."

Rex McKay raised a hand and brushed his mustache. "You a friend of Enoch Lee's?" he challenged abruptly.

"Never saw him."

"Then ride with us and be damned to your business with an old psalm singer. We're turnin' back in a little while."

"I'll ride after when I'm through at the Wagon Wheel," Sundown stated coolly.

Rex McKay let out an explosive oath. His face twisted in ugly lines. "McKay men take orders!" he said angrily. "I tell you not to go to that Wagon Wheel ranch house. Mebbe you're Sundown Daly, an' mebbe not. I ain't takin' chances."

Salty O'Shea said softly: "He's Daly all right. An' he's fixin' to join the McKays. He got a raw deal in Las Piedras two years ago. He never kilt that deputy. Hughie Jennings ain't sendin' a man to us unless he's all right. It's gettin' dark. We'll be through in a little while. What's to stop us from ridin' on to the ranch house with him? We can wait until his business is done an' take him back with us."

Rex McKay rubbed the palm of his right hand slowly over the top of the saddle horn and considered. Suddenly snapping his fingers, he decided: "We'll do that. Come on, ride with us, Daly."

IV

"THE NOOSE"

Sundown rode along. The men were not unfriendly. Rather, they ignored him. There were three of them now besides Salty O'Shea. Five men, scattered out in the gathering darkness, drifting a seasonable bunch of yearlings before them.

Now and then one of the men detached himself and drove several of the yearlings off from the main body, rushing them out of sight, returning empty-handed each time. They repeated this move again and again, without looking to Rex McKay for orders.

Puzzled, Sundown rode and held his counsel. They were on Wagon Wheel land. They were drifting Wagon Wheel yearlings as he had noted by the brand. They were heading deeper into Wagon Wheel range, and, instead of rounding up the yearlings, they were scattering them out.

Had they been rustling Wagon Wheel beef, Sundown would have understood it. Had they been heading toward the hills and keeping the small herd compact, it would have made sense. This did not. He did not ask.

In half an hour the last of the yearlings were scattered. The riders gathered about Rex McKay. It was almost dark now. The big fellow's face was barely visible as he said casually to them: "Here's a man to take Hughie Jennings's place, boys. He's riding to the Wagon Wheel for a little business. We'll side him for comp'ny an' take 'im back with us. Daly's his name. Sundown Daly. He's been in the pen with Hughie Jennings."

That was all. No comments were made. But as they rode through the night, Sundown sensed the riders were close about him, ready, he guessed, to see that he made no attempt to break away. He was not accepted as one of them, despite Rex McKay's words.

Sundown ignored it. He could understand their caution, but he wondered about the dead man back on Cowpen Creek. Why had he been killed? Who was he? What were these McKays up to?

They topped a rise of ground. Dimly lighted windows were visible a quarter of a mile away. A dog barked, fell silent.

Rex McKay said in an emotionless voice: "There's the Wagon Wheel headquarters. I don't reckon you'll be long, Daly?"

"Can't tell. Be back when I'm through," Sundown said shortly.

"Better leave your guns with us," Rex McKay said in the same detached manner. "Bad things to be carryin' on a friendly call. They might misunderstand you."

Sundown said dryly: "I doubt it. I'll take 'em. I'm partial to 'em."

The men were crowded close about him in the darkness. He heard a stir behind. Without warning, the hard muzzle of a rifle touched his back. Salty O'Shea said mildly: "Red wants 'em, friend. You wouldn't disappoint him, would you?"

"When you put it that way," said Sundown gently over his shoulder, "I wouldn't. But someday soon, Salty, old friend, we'll powwow over your rambunctiousness. You're too free with a gun to suit my taste."

"Shore," said Salty affably. "Always ready to talk over little things like that. Meanwhile, jest hold still an' easy while the boys get your hardware."

Rex McKay chuckled softly as guns were slipped from holsters. "You'll learn to take orders if you trail with the McKays," he commented. "We'll be waitin' here for you, Daly."

Sundown rode toward the Wagon Wheel lights.

A chorus of barks and snarls greeted him as he came to the low adobe building that was obviously the ranch house. An open door let a shaft of light out on a *portal.* A man stood framed there, peering into the night. "Who is it?" he called gruffly.

"Stranger," said Sundown. "I'm lookin' for Jordan Lee."

"Light an' come in."

Sundown dismounted, untied the saddlebags, walking toward the *portal* with them. As he approached, the man disappeared. His voice could be heard calling the girl.

She stood framed in the doorway a moment later, peering out at him questioningly. Sundown felt himself growing speechless, awkward as he looked at her.

Jordan, her father had called her, after a river across the seas, and she was like a river, this girl who stood in the doorway with the light behind her. A river, smooth and clear with soft curves and unexpected depth beneath the beauty of the surface. A river, flowing gently and easily, with the capacity to become a raging torrent. That was Jordan Lee as Sundown saw her first. Height barely to his shoulders. Brown hair waved softly and close to her head. Her eyes, dark and questioning, in a young face that was oddly mature.

"You wish to see me?" she asked.

Sundown grinned at her. For the moment bitterness left him and he forgot the past. Forgot the Red McKays, the outlaw brand he wore. "If you're Jordan Lee, I brought these saddlebags to you," he said. Sundown held them out.

She took them in slender, strong hands that were no strangers to work. Eyebrows lifting in a puzzled frown, she said: "For me? Why?"

Awkwardness descended on Sundown again at the pain he was about to bring her. "They're your brother's, Mark Lee's. He asked me to bring them to you."

Her face lightened with eagerness. "Mark! Where is he?"

Sundown stumbled over it. He had never done a harder thing. "He's . . . you see . . . I hate to bring you the news . . . he's dead," Sundown said heavily.

The joy and eagerness fled from her face. Disbelief, grief, misery came then. Her hands trembled. She swayed. He thought she was about to fall, and put out a hand. But she drew a deep breath and was the master of herself once more.

"Come in," she said.

Sundown, who should have been on his way at once, followed her into the house. He found himself in a large room with polished tree trunks across the ceiling. Deer hides, bearskins, and Navajo rugs were on the floor. A great stone fireplace was built into the back wall. There were books about, lithograph prints on the walls.

Jordan Lee laid the saddlebags on the table, and looked at him. Her eyes were glistening, her face pale.

"Tell me," she commanded.

Sundown lied bravely. "A horse, miss. Hadn't been broke right. He fell over backwards on Mark. It was over in a minute. He asked me to bring the saddlebags to you, and to tell you he always thought you was a fine sister, even if he hadn't said much about it."

It was hard going. She questioned him. Sundown lied with a straight face as he told of the happening down south, near the border. She listened, hanging onto his words. When he finished, she said brokenly: "Poor Mark. I can't believe he's dead."

A harsh voice behind Sundown exclaimed: "Mark's dead! What talk is this?"

The door had opened soundlessly in time for her words to be overheard. Sundown had seen Enoch Lee before. There was no change now—the same stern, ascetic face, with cold eyes under bushy black brows. The same stubbly chin beard and mustache, graying slightly now. A stern man, upright, righteous according to his convictions. An honest man, without fear. Harsh to the breaking point with those who transgressed the code by which he lived. Enoch Lee demanded again, loudly, of them both: "What is it about Mark? Who is this man, Jordan?"

Jordan Lee pointed to the saddlebags. "Mark's, Dad. He sent them by this man before he died. It was down near the border. A horse fell on him."

"That's right." Sundown nodded to Enoch Lee's fierce look of inquiry. "I was there. He was a good boy, hard-working, steady. We all liked him. And now I'll be going, if you don't mind. I rode out of my way, and I'll have to be getting back."

A cool, amused voice at the door where Enoch Lee had been said: "It's a good story, Daly, but it won't work. Put your hands up! You're traveling into Las Piedras with me. Sheriff Wallace wants you for murder!"

Sundown swung around, hands instinctively lifting from his sides to show that he was unarmed. He recognized the voice before he saw the man and found he was right. It was Yance Claggett, standing there in the doorway with a big Frontier model Colt in his hand. Yance Claggett, big and debonair as ever, handsome, too. For a day's ride in any direction there were no finer-looking men than the Claggett brothers, Yance and Gil. Yance was the older, and he was not more than thirty-five. Sinuous where Sundown was powerful, smooth-tongued where Sundown was blunt. A man of ready laughter, of shrewd deals that somehow bred no animosity, Yance Claggett was well on his way to wealth. He bought cattle, traded ranch land, owned the biggest saloon in Las Piedras, had scattered interests that were not public knowledge. There had been bad blood between him and Sundown for years.

Yance Claggett's smooth-shaven, handsome face was smiling slightly behind the level gun. But his eyes were flaming watchfully.

The bitter lines settled in Sundown's face once more. His eyes became coldly blank, his voice expressionless. "I'm not armed," he pointed out.

"Put 'em up!" said Yance Claggett. "You're a tricky one, Daly. You've probably got a Derringer stuck around you some place, like that fellow over by Paradise yesterday."

"What is this, Yance?" Enoch Lee questioned brusquely. "This man seems to have brought news of Mark's death. Do you know him?"

"Every inch of his worthless hide," Yance Claggett stated smoothly. "His name is Sundown Daly. Remember his trial two years ago for shooting Tom Means, the deputy? He just got out of prison several days ago. He hasn't been near the border in years. He an' another man held up the stage over by Paradise yesterday afternoon. They killed one of the passengers and made their escape. Sheriff Wallace got Daly's description this afternoon and recognized it. I was in his office at the time. Wallace was at the prison when Daly left, and tells me Daly said then he was turning outlaw. I don't know what brings him here, but I'll take him in to Wallace."

Jordan Lee had looked startled at sight of Claggett's gun. She stood rigidly, questioningly, while he spoke. Now she said in an unsteady voice: "But he brought Mark's saddle-bags."

She opened them swiftly, emptied the contents on the table as she finished speaking. Two small canvas bags of coin chinked heavily. There was a packet of old letters, a razor, two pairs of socks. Not much. A few pitiful personal possessions. The canvas sacks held only silver dollars when she opened them.

"That's my razor that Mark took when he left," Enoch Lee said in a dead, brittle voice. His stern face might have been carved from rock. His voice broke, unsteady for an instant. "My razor . . . my boy! And . . . and this man, Daly, and another held up the stage yesterday?"

Yance Claggett nodded. "One of them was shot with a Derringer and wounded badly. Daly here knows," he said, "what happened to the man who was with him."

Enoch Lee turned on Sundown with all the fury of a prophet of old.

"You led my boy into a thing like that!" he blazed. "He was young, willful, wild! A man like you could sway him!"

"Hold on!" Sundown protested. "You're on the wrong trail, mister."

"Damn your black heart!" Enoch Lee thundered. "I'll take you in to the sheriff myself! I'll be standing there when they put a noose around your neck and spring the trap! Verily, vengeance shall be mine!"

Sundown looked at Jordan Lee. What Yance Claggett thought did not matter. Enoch Lee's righteous anger was in keeping with the man's character. But somehow he wanted this clear-eyed girl to understand. She was standing white-faced, her form stiff, straight. Her eyes were hard with scorn.

"So it was all lies!" she said. "A horse didn't fall on Mark. He was shot while holding up the stage and killing a man. You went from prison to *that!* And then came here with lies on your lips. Couldn't you even be honest about . . . death?"

Yance Claggett stood there soberly, but dancing lights of satisfaction gleamed in his eyes as he looked at Sundown, and then spoke to her.

"I'm sorry, dear. I should have kept quiet. But when I heard his little story, I couldn't keep still. Leave us with him and we'll handle him."

"No, Yance. I . . . I'm all right."

Yance Claggett had made a conquest, not the first Sundown knew about. Somehow this one irritated him. She was too good for Claggett, and always would be. A man could look at her and know it.

Enoch Lee said harshly: "I'll get some of the boys out of the bunkhouse."

Claggett lifted a protesting hand. "No need of that. You won't even have to ride in. I'm a deputy. I can handle him. I'll put a rope around his neck."

Sundown, catching the grim note of satisfaction in Yance Claggett's voice, knew that he had small chance of getting into town alive. Claggett had him put out of the way two years ago. Claggett was afraid of him. This golden opportunity was made to order. Even should he reach Las Piedras, he would probably be sentenced to hang in short order. The facts were too damning.

None of that showed on Sundown Daly's face. He was cold, deliberate, as he looked at Yance Claggett and Enoch Lee and let his gaze wander around the room. Rex McKay had his guns. He damned the big, red-faced outlaw to himself.

Enoch Lee said grudgingly: "If you can get him in alone, Yance, go ahead. It's late to be ridin' into town an' back. I'll come in tomorrow."

Then Sundown saw the looped end of a cartridge belt showing over the arm of a rocking chair upholstered in horsehair at the end of the room. He could not see the holster from where he stood, but cartridges were in the belt loops. It was reasonable that the gun would be in the holster. It was a full twenty feet away, past the table where Mark Lee's saddlebags lay in the light of a big, nickel-finished oil lamp.

Sundown shrugged helplessly, said to Yance Claggett: "Looks like you're running this show. I'll have my day in court. Before I leave, here's something Miss Lee had better see."

He stepped to the table and picked up the packet of letters and in the same motion he swept the lamp off the table and dropped to the floor. Claggett's gun shattered the quiet of the room.

V

"DEATH'S HEAD MINE"

The bullet grazed Sundown's shoulder as he went down behind the table. The glass lamp shade and chimney crashed into bits on the floor. The lamp flickered, went out, plunging the room into pitch blackness. Claggett's gun roared three more times as Sundown hurled himself away from the table across the floor. Lead raked into the table, smacked into the floor behind him.

Sundown's outstretched fingers struck the rough horse-hair upholstery of the chair—found the gun belt—found the holster on the chair seat. He jerked the weapon out, sprang up with ringing ears as Claggett's shots ceased.

Powder smoke was rank in the room, mixed with the reek of spilled oil and the charred wick. Claggett's excited voice said loudly: "If I didn't get 'im, then I will soon as I see him! Jordan, are you all right?"

She answered from before the big stone fireplace: "All right, Yance. Did . . . did you kill him?"

"I hope so," Claggett replied. "He's a bad one."

Empty shells struck the floor near Sundown. He heard Claggett's thumbing fresh ones in. Assuming his man was unarmed and probably wounded, Claggett was being reckless. Sundown moved forward noiselessly toward the table. Matches flared brightly in Enoch Lee's hand.

Yance Claggett's handsome face stood out sharply. A spasm of surprise crossed it, and quick, panicky fear as Claggett looked into the muzzle of the gun, and past it at the mirthless grin on Sundown's face.

"Drop it!" Sundown rapped out.

"Yance, watch out!" Jordan Lee cried.

Enoch Lee stood rooted to the floor, three bunched matches blazing in his fingers. Yance Claggett's gun jerked up, shot.

Sundown felt the bullet strike his side violently, tearing through cloth and flesh. He shot an instant later. Yance Claggett staggered as the gun spun from his fingers and thudded to the floor. He cried out in pain. Enoch flicked the matches out, dodging from the spot where he was standing.

Blackness closed in about them once more, but Sundown was already around the end of the table. Two long strides and he found Claggett, who was still cursing as he bent, searching for his gun. Sundown caught a handful of heavy black hair, jerked him up, jammed his gun in Claggett's middle.

"Easy on it," he snapped. "Let's have some light before I get nervous an' plug this good-lookin' snake!"

"Strike a light quick, Enoch!" Yance Claggett gasped. "He'll do it!"

Matches flared once more. Yance Claggett's face was a pain-twisted mask, a grimace of fear.

In a quick little rush Jordan Lee reached his side. She caught Claggett's arm, blazing at Sundown: "There's been enough of this! Get back! You . . . you shall not shoot him!" The placid river had, indeed, become a torrent. Her anger was beautiful, reckless, unheeding.

"Jordan, get back!" Enoch Lee cried hoarsely.

Yance Claggett said nothing at first. Blood was dripping from his fingers. His face showed fear, and now bewilderment. He had tried to kill, and he expected the same.

The matches burned low in Enoch Lee's fingers. Sundown stepped back, bent, and snatched Claggett's gun from the floor. He laughed as the blackness fell about them again.

"Take him!" he said to Jordan Lee. "Hide him behind your skirts! Let him lie to you. A woman can't see the dust for the smoke she raises when she falls in love. Enoch Lee, you Bible-shoutin' old hypocrite, your boy made a wrong step, but he died like a man. If Yance Claggett takes his place, don't look for the same. He's a different breed."

"I'll have you hunted down like a dog!" Enoch Lee said harshly in the darkness.

Sundown laughed. "Miss Jordan, are them your sentiments?"

"I hope," said Jordan Lee passionately, "you get all you deserve!"

"That would be poison to your pretty boy," Sundown chuckled. "I'm wishin' you good luck with him. You'll need it."

He stepped out on the *portal,* closing the door behind him. How many men had been within earshot he had no way of knowing. As he left the *portal,* men came running around the end of the house. Sundown ran for the black, caught reins and saddle horn, and swung up.

A loud voice demanded: "What's all the shootin' about?"

"Trouble inside. Enoch Lee wants you."

"Hey, where are you going?" the voice demanded as the black wheeled and leaped to the rake of spurs. "Who are you?"

Enoch Lee's voice shouted from the front door: *"Stop him!"*

Guns barked loudly. Bullets whined closely. Sundown emptied one revolver back at them, and rode hard, leaning low.

The five men were waiting where he had left them. Rex McKay hailed him as he galloped up. "What's happened? We heard shots?"

Sundown reined up by the speaker.

"Gimme my guns!" he demanded in cold fury.

They were returned.

"What happened?" Rex McKay demanded again.

"My business! An' the next man who asks for my guns'll get trouble instead! Your damn' foolishness almost put a rope around my neck! Ride on if I'm goin' with you!"

They obeyed him. His cold fury and manner held them silent as they rode off into the night. Even Rex McKay held his tongue.

They rode fast and far, back into the hills, the mountains, along trails strange and unknown to Sundown. They threaded the pines of the upper slopes, traversed narrow, deep-walled cañons, coming finally to a high, windswept shelf on the upper slopes.

The dark loom of buildings bulked in the waning starlight. Lighted windows gave life to the deserted night, and the tangle of pines, aspen, and undergrowth formed a leafy wall on three sides of the open space. They came to it out of a narrow defile, and Sundown knew where he was. Long ago gangs of men had mined silver and gold from this high mountain shelf. It was the Death's Head Mine, so-called because a grinning white skull had been found on the original vein outcropping.

The gold had played out. Silver had dropped in price. The mine and all the surface buildings had been abandoned for many years, and here the Red McKays were nesting, like eagles in a mountain aerie.

They stopped before a two-story building that had been a saloon and boarding house for the miners. It was a big, gaunt, frame pile. They tramped across porch floors that creaked underfoot, entering a long front room that had been bar and lobby. The bar glass was cracked, gaping blank in spots. The floor was dark with the grime of years. Cobwebs and age lay thick on every side, but the tables and chairs were still in place, and the ornate brass chandelier lamp was burning over the bar.

Five men were playing poker at a big, round table. They greeted the newcomers with boisterous salutations, eying Sundown narrowly. Every man was armed. They were a hard-boiled lot.

Sundown had only a moment to look them over. A high-pitched voice called: "Who's that with you, Rex?"

At the end of the room, stairs led up to the second floor. The speaker was on a lower landing, legs braced apart, hands hooked in a gun belt, head bent forward in inquiry. Spindle-shanked, pot-bellied, pink-cheeked, with a glistening bald skull fringed by coarse red hair, he looked not more than forty. The Red McKays terrorized a vast expanse of range country, and Jupiter McKay, their leader, would have made a stranger laugh at first sight. Sundown did not laugh. He knew too much about the man.

What mattered the bandy legs and pot belly, the feminine voice and pink cheeks? Sundown's eyes marked the lean, powerful hands hooked on the gun belt, the tight-lipped mouth, the cold eyes staring fixedly under coarse red eyebrows.

Hughie Jennings had told him what other men had paid dearly to learn. Jupiter McKay was tireless in the saddle, swift, powerful in action, a dead shot. For all his thin voice he was harsh, cruel when necessary, iron-willed, cunning.

Rex McKay said meekly as he walked with Sundown to the steps: "He's Sundown Daly that Hughie Jennings wrote about. He says a posse's after him, an' he was headin' here."

"So," said Jupiter McKay mildly, "Daly, eh?" His eyes drilled Sundown. His tight lips pursed thoughtfully, smiled suddenly. "Glad to see you, Daly. We can always use a good man. Rex'll give you a room upstairs. We're livin' in style just now. There's grub in the kitchen. Black Sam'll feed you."

It was a simple as that. Rex McKay led him up to a little cubby-hole room. It held a rickety old chair and a cot; blankets were rustled for him. A grinning black giant in the kitchen downstairs warmed him a plate of grub.

Other men drifted in and out of the big room during the next hour. Fifteen or twenty of them, Sundown judged. Horses were corralled at the back of the building. No women were about. The Red McKays were a compact, mobile group that moved far and fast when occasion warranted.

Sundown turned in early. He lay for a time, thinking of that rider who had died on Cowpen Creek. He had known the Red McKays dealt in death and terror. He had been willing to accept it, but shooting a fleeing man in the back was different. Sundown's last thoughts were of Jordan Lee, and her blazing anger.

VI

"BLOTTED BRANDS"

The new day was clear, sunny, peaceful. The front of the clearing dropped a thousand sheer feet into an abyss. One looked off a hundred and fifty miles over the rolling range country to hazy purple mountains on the horizon. There was a certain activity going on today. Men came and went on mysterious errands. In the evening they played cards, drank moderately, talked, even sang, and yet one felt the ever-present tension in the air. They lived with death and violence, and it marked them and their actions.

Few questions were asked of Sundown. No hostility was shown after Jupiter McKay accepted him. The next afternoon Sundown saddled the black and rode out unchallenged. High-frowning walls bounded the narrow defile through which he had entered the clearing, forming an impregnable gate to this lair of the McKays. It would be a bold posse that would try to fight through—and it was the only way in from the lower country.

Two guards on duty at the entrance waved at him. One of them called: "The old man's down there somewheres! If you see him, tell him Mike Reeder rode in a little while ago!"

"I'll look for him," Sundown promised.

He rode slowly down an ancient road, badly eroded. Birds flashed through the trees. A doe bounded across the road ahead. Sundown grinned, then breathed deeply. This was freedom.

He watched for Jupiter McKay. Three miles down the road he saw a big white stallion tied in a grassy clearing. A second horse stood beside it. Sundown rode there, looking about.

Jupiter McKay was not in sight. A narrow path led back into the brush. Somewhere nearby a small waterfall poured musically. Sundown followed the path. He walked perhaps fifty yards—and stopped abruptly, drawing back into the shelter of a bush.

Sunlight dappled the grassy bank at the base of the waterfall. Two men were sitting there, smoking, talking. Jupiter McKay and Yance Claggett!

Neither had seen him. Their words were audible. Jupiter McKay's high-pitched voice was saying tartly: "You got no kick comin', Claggett. Rex figgered you might be in the house, an' sent 'im up without his guns. If you couldn't handle him, it's your own fault."

Yance Claggett spat, swore. "He was too tricky for me. Now you've got him, an' it's up to you. I don't want him around. He's dangerous. Get rid of him, or have him turned over to the sheriff."

Jupiter McKay laughed, tossed his sombrero to the ground, ran his fingers through that belligerent red fringe about his bald head. "Plenty of time for that. He's not lookin' for trouble. What about the Wagon Wheel? I'm tired of waiting. I've done my part, an' now it's up to you."

Claggett shrugged. "They started their roundup yesterday. I've already advanced the old man five thousand on his beef. Soon as they're in the shipping pens, I'll set off the fireworks. Got it all arranged. Won't be any trouble. That'll give us the Wagon Wheel and a clear way through to Surprise Cañon. I'll be able to handle all the beef you can throw in on Wagon Wheel range. We'll both be sitting pretty."

"What about Lee's girl?" Jupiter McKay asked slyly.

Claggett grinned. "She'll go with the deal. I know where I stand. Now about this Daly. Are you sure you can handle him? He'll make trouble if he gets half a chance."

Jupiter McKay raised a sinewy fist, brought his fingers together in a crushing grip. "Like that," he said. "Forget about him."

Sundown moved into the open. "Stand up, you bald-headed old curly wolf, while I cut your toe nails!" he said aloud.

They came upright, grabbing for their guns. One look at Sundown's crouching figure behind his level belt guns was enough. Their hands shot in the air. Claggett cursed softly. Jupiter McKay blinked, forced a smile, said heartily: "Hello, Daly. Havin' a little fun? Put up them guns an' set down."

Sundown walked slowly to them, holstering one gun. "I made a mistake," he said through his teeth. "I thought I was comin' into good clean company when I headed for the McKays. I knew you was buzzards, but I didn't figger you'd eat your own meat. Unbuckle your belts an' chuck 'em on the ground."

Jupiter McKay's face reddened, his cold eyes under the coarse red brows gleaming. "Daly, I've had about enough of this. Git on your hoss an' ride if you don't like the McKays!"

"I'm ridin'," Sundown agreed, "but I'll pluck your tail feathers first. Jump, you pot-bellied old buzzard!"

Yance Claggett's right hand was bandaged heavily. With the left he unbuckled his gun belt and tossed it on the ground. Jupiter McKay hesitated, then slowly did the same. His eyes never left Sundown's face. His thin, bloodless lips barely moved. "You're a dead man now, Daly! No man ever did this to me an' lived to tell about it! I'll have you ridden down an' dragged behind a hoss!"

"I know," said Sundown. "You're a bad actor. But right now I'm poison! Walk out to your horses, gents. An' don't look so green about the gills. I don't shoot men in the back."

They went unwillingly. A lariat was tied to Jupiter McKay's saddle.

"Climb on an' hang your belly across the saddle," Sundown ordered Jupiter McKay. "Claggett here'll tie you on so you won't fall off."

Jupiter McKay began to swear in rising fury. It did him no good. In the end he was forced to climb awkwardly over his saddle, head and shoulders hanging down on one side, legs on the other.

Claggett, white-faced, took the lariat reluctantly and tied him. Sundown looked on with grim humor, inspected the job critically, then nodded with satisfaction.

"You look like a haunch of bad meat," he said to Jupiter McKay's purpling face. "Some of your men will ride by an' find you before long. Claggett, fork your horse and smoke down the trail ahead of me."

"What are you going to do?" Yance Claggett asked through stiff lips.

"I don't know," Sundown confessed, "but it'll probably be plenty before I'm through. I can't stomach your breed, and McKay here's almost as bad. Get going, Claggett!"

It was two hours later before Sundown and Claggett stopped before a small log cabin in the foothills. Their horses were blowing. They had ridden hard down the rough mountain trails. Claggett shifted stiffly in the saddle and asked: "Now what?"

"Light," said Sundown briefly. Gun in hand, he waited until Claggett stood by his horse's head, then swung out of the saddle himself. "Inside," he ordered.

The door was unlocked. A faint look of hope on Claggett's face died away as they entered and found the interior deserted. A rough bunk in one corner, frying pan and coffee pot, and a shelf of canned goods over a small sheet-iron stove comprised the major furnishings.

"Saw this the other day," said Sundown. "Figgered it was a line rider's cabin. Everyone'll be at the roundup now, and we can make ourselves at home. Climb on that bunk, Claggett."

Yance Claggett's sullen face darkened with anger. "This has gone far enough!" he exclaimed furiously. "What are you up to?"

Sundown grinned at him. "You'd be surprised. Get on that bunk. Should be some spare rope around here."

In a box that served for a table and catch-all, he found a lariat that had been broken, spliced, broken again, and discarded and several worn pigging strings. With the pigging strings he tied Claggett's ankles, his wrists and elbows behind him. If these knots were loose, he apparently did not notice.

"Now wiggle an' squall till you get a frog in your throat," he commented.

Claggett suddenly looked haggard, no longer debonair. "Let me go," he begged. "I'll bargain with you."

"You're wigglin' quick," said Sundown.

Claggett suddenly seemed to realize that talk was wasted. Apprehension increased on his face. "This won't help you any," he said. "There's over four hundred dollars in my pocket. Take it an' leave the country. I'll keep my mouth shut."

"I'll bet you will," said Sundown. "An' then gobble up the Wagon Wheel. You won't get it, Claggett. You've been crooked long enough. I figgered on turnin' outlaw . . . but it only turned my stomach. I've elected myself a deputy, an' I'm goin' to raise hell on the Las Piedras range till you hunt for a hole an' crawl in it. You an' the McKays."

"You'll be hanged so quick you won't know what happened if you stay around here, Daly."

"First off," said Sundown, "I'm going into Las Piedras an' get your brother Gil. He'll talk quicker than you. I'm going to take him to the Wagon Wheel an' pull the truth out of him before Enoch Lee. When the old man hears your brother talk, he'll hit the warpath. You'll be finished then. Figger that out while you're takin' the rest cure here."

Sundown went outside, unsaddled Claggett's horse, and ran it off. Taking the broken lariat, he rode off.

Wagon Wheel cattle were soon in evidence. He looked over each bunch and rode on. In the head of a small draw half a dozen cows, calves and two yearlings, were grazing. Sundown spurred toward one of the yearlings.

He had crudely spliced the rope as he rode, making it fast

to the saddle horn. The black rushed the frightened yearling through a tangle of brush, down into a dry arroyo bed, and closed in swiftly. An underhand cast to a hind leg and the yearling went down in a tangled heap as the black stopped short.

Sundown lit running, caught the other hind leg, and flipped the yearling over, revealing the brand. He studied it intently, passing his hand over it, and straightened, frowning to himself.

He rolled a cigarette, flicked a match with a thumbnail, and inhaled. Without warning a crisp, even voice ordered: "I'm covering you, Daly! Don't move!"

It was Jordan Lee speaking. She had emerged from a tangle of piñon and brush on the right arroyo bank above him. She stood there, slim, straight, eyeing him along the motionless barrel of a .30-30 carbine.

The sun wrinkles at the corners of Sundown's eyes deepened as he lifted his hands, smiling thinly. "It's like wishing for an angel and having one drop out of the sky," he said. "I was thinking of you."

He was close enough to see the color leap into her cheeks. He saw her lip curl with scorn. "What are you doing with that calf?" she demanded.

Sundown looked at it, at her. "Trying out my arm," he said. "Got him neat the first throw. Step down an' be sociable, Miss Jordan. Your arm'll get tired holding that gun."

She wore soft leather boots, a divided riding skirt, and a short buckskin jacket. Her head was bare. Flying tendrils of hair framed her face, and she was taut, angry, threatening.

"I'm coming down!" she flared. "And I'm going to take your guns away and herd you in to the sheriff! I'll shoot you if your hands drop below your ears before I say to!"

"They won't," Sundown assured her gallantly. "They're hooked right up there in the air, miss. You don't need a gun to keep 'em there."

She came down the bank cautiously, stepped to him, holding the carbine steady. Sundown turned his back obligingly. She plucked the guns from his holsters. He chuckled over his shoulder at her. "You do it like an old hand," he said approvingly. "Now can I haul my fists down?"

"Step away from me before you do. And, remember, I'll shoot you with less provocation than you killed Dan Steele two days ago."

Sundown moved three paces away, lowered his arms slowly, and faced her with a quick frown. "Dan Steele? I don't know him."

"One of our hands," she said. "He was riding circle day before yesterday. His horse came in without him in the night. We found Dan at Cowpen Creek this morning, shot in the back."

"I see," said Sundown softly.

"I see, too!" she blazed. "Dan was a hard worker. Steady. He was to be married next month. You shot him in the back and came to me with lies about my brother! Oh, don't bother to deny it!" she said scornfully as Sundown started to speak. "They backtracked on your trail. Your horse had one crooked hind shoe. They found its mark beside Dan Steele's body. When I think of Dan's girl crying her heart out, I could drop you where you stand!"

Cheeks flaming, voice shaking with anger, she was beautiful as she stood there. She was not afraid of him. She despised him.

Sundown drew a deep breath, smiled crookedly. "Put up your gun, Jordan Lee," he told her. "I've been to prison, and I'm accused of murder. Another one don't matter much, I guess. I happened to see your man shot, but I didn't have a hand in it. I couldn't have saved him. If your men looked close, they found other tracks beside him. Why should I shoot a man I never saw before . . . and then come on to tell you about your brother?"

"You shot him because you were afraid of him!" she retorted swiftly. "You knew men were looking for you."

"Shot him in the back while he ran away from me?" Sundown asked dryly. "And then came on to your house where your hands could grab me? You reason like a woman. I'm no good, so I naturally have to be guilty. Put up that gun and tell me why the Wagon Wheel is rustling cattle."

Her mouth opened soundlessly. Then fresh anger swept her. "What do you mean?" she demanded.

Sundown grinned at her. "This yearling is wearing a Wagon Wheel brand. Look close and you'll see someone has blotted a Double Anchor into the Wagon Wheel. It's peeled and healed, but you can still tell the fresh parts from the old."

Sundown knelt, drew two quarter circles in the sand with his finger, and connected them with a straight line. "Double Anchor," he explained. With a circular motion he turned the two quarter circles into one full circle. Two more lines through it made a six-spoked wagon wheel. "That's how it was done," he said, straightening. "The Double Anchor range is north of you. Ben Salazar used to own it. Who holds it now?"

She stared at the brand he had drawn in the sand, then turned to the yearling and studied the brand on its hip. Her watchfulness had not abated, but she seemed worried, uncertain.

"Wallace, the sheriff, owns the Double Anchor now," she said slowly. "He bought it from Salazar about two years ago. We haven't bought any cattle from him. I . . . I don't understand it. Who did this?"

"Wallace will ask that," Sundown told her. "There's a lot of these blotted brands among your beef. It's clumsy work, and too fresh to pass. When it shows up at the roundup, there'll be trouble. They'll say your old man is a rustler."

"No one will believe it!" she flamed.

Sundown shrugged. "They'll believe what they see."

By the swift misery flooding her face, he saw she was convinced. All the anger was gone from her now. She looked suddenly frightened.

"It would kill him!" she burst out. "Everything we have is here on the ranch. Dad has fought and worked for it. The last few years he's been almost at the end of his rope. Everyone knows it. They'll . . . they'll think he rustled cattle to keep his head above water."

Sundown prodded: "What makes you so sure he didn't do it?"

Her chin lifted proudly. Her eyes scorned him. "He's my father. I know him!"

"Too bad you don't know me as well," said Sundown calmly. He bent, loosened the rope, watching the yearling bolt off along the arroyo. He coiled the rope, dropped it over his saddle horn, turned to her. "The McKay gang did this," he told her. "Day before yesterday I watched them run these yearlings in on your land. They shot your man. I guess he cut their trail, and they wanted to shut his mouth. That's what brought me back today. I couldn't figger why the McKays would be bringing cattle *onto* your range."

"You're a strange man," she said. "I don't understand you or the things you do. But I believe you. You couldn't have had a hand in this. Get out and don't come back."

She dropped his guns in the sand, and turned away.

"Wait a minute!" Sundown said sharply. He picked up his

guns, asking as she turned back toward him: "What are you going to do?"

"Find Father at once and have him go to the sheriff at once."

"Yance Claggett is thick with the sheriff, isn't he?"

"What has that got to do with it?" Her eyes smoldered.

"Nothing," Sundown denied hastily. "But if Wallace knows about this, he'll laugh at your father."

"Why shouldn't the sheriff know about this?"

"Your father owes money. If word gets around he's a rustler, they'll come down hard on him. He'll lose the ranch. Maybe Wallace wants more land. He may be mixed up in this."

"Dad would fight!" she said furiously.

"Wouldn't do him any good. Wallace is backed by the law. If the McKay gang is hooked up with the sheriff, your old man is bucking a stacked deck. My story won't help. They'd swear I was lying. Where's your father?"

"At the house."

"You better go to your father," said Sundown. "Tell him about the blotted brands. Have him call his men in from the roundup. Tell him I warned you. The McKays are riding today. They're playing for the Wagon Wheel. No telling what will happen."

"What are you going to do?"

Sundown grinned at her. "If anyone asks you, tell 'em I'll be at the Wagon Wheel sometime this evening."

VII

"SATAN'S DEPUTY"

You came down off the mesa through a welter of great rocks, frost-riven, weather-worn, and Las Piedras was there, flung along the rocky bank of Monterey Creek. The stores and saloons, the bank, and eating place of Fat Lee's, the wizened Chinaman, were all there in a cluster not more than two hundred yards long. At the end of the street, under towering cottonwoods, was the shabby little courthouse. Las Piedras was the county seat.

It was twilight when Sundown rode off the mesa, and the shadows were even longer in Las Piedras. Lights were burning behind windows. Horses were racked before stores and saloons, but there were few people in the open.

He rode slowly along the street, unrecognized. For a moment he paused before a small frame building whose front window bore the legend: **Claggett Land and Cattle Company.** The office inside was dark. Sundown rode on along the street to the courthouse. His face grew hard as he looked at the two-story brick building, with jail and sheriff's office on the ground floor. There, two years ago, he had sat through a trial and heard sentence passed on him. Many things had happened since.

Sundown turned to the right, passed the cottonwoods on the courthouse lawn, up the slope of the hillside. Beyond, straggled out for a quarter of a mile, were small adobe houses and gardens with, now and then, a small picket corral. A two-story frame house beyond the courthouse grounds was his destination. A light was burning inside. A dog barked as he rode to the side of the house and dismounted.

In the back a door slammed, feet crunched. A short, swarthy Mexican came out of the gathering dusk and peered at him.

"Gil Claggett inside?" Sundown asked.

"No, *señor*. *Señor* Claggett ees at hees saloon, I theenk."

"I want to see him . . . here," said Sundown. "Here's a half a dollar. Tell him, and then buy yourself a drink."

"*Gracias, señor*. You weel come eenside to wait? I am thee house man."

Sundown smiled grimly in the dim light. "Sure. It's all the same."

The Mexican escorted him to the front door, showed him into a small parlor where an oil lamp burned beneath a great shade. The Mexican was swart, dark, with Indian blood showing in his coarse features. His eyes were alert, shrewd, his bow ingratiating.

"You please to estay here, an' I weel get thee *Señor* Claggett," he promised, hat in hand.

"Sure. And don't stop to buy your drink before you get him," Sundown stated as the Mexican hurried out.

He rolled a cigarette, paced back and forth for several minutes, smoking, and then swung on his heel and went outside. Minute by minute it was getting darker. The aromatic smell of cedar smoke from kitchen fires hung low, pungent. Sundown slipped his guns from the holsters and inspected them.

The front porch of the Claggett house was almost hidden by a screen of morning glory vines. Sundown went into the blackest corner of the porch and took up his position. He was waiting there, silent, invisible, when a man reached the porch steps on his toes and came up almost inaudibly. It was Gil Claggett, almost as big as his brother Yance. Instead of opening the door and entering, Gil tiptoed to the parlor windows and peered in. He seemed puzzled at seeing no one inside, pressed his face closer to the glass to see better.

Sundown spoke softly. "You're wastin' time, Gil. I figgered you'd do something like that." He closed the space between them as he spoke. His left hand snapped out, knocked Gil Claggett's hand from the gun butt to which it had streaked. His right shoved a gun in Claggett's middle. "Take it easy," he advised. "I don't want to kill you before you get a chance to talk an' save your dirty hide!"

The swift intake of Gil Claggett's breath was audible. Rigid, he peered.

"It's me, Sundown Daly. I reckon you and Yance knew I'd show up one of these days."

Gil Claggett's voice came hoarse. "What do you want, Daly?"

"You," said Sundown. "Where's Yance?"

"Don't know. He rode out today on some business."

"I know," said Sundown gently. "I left him hog-tied in a little cabin up in the foothills. He's tamed and full of talk, Gil, and he ain't here to help you tonight. I'll tell you what he already knows. You Claggetts are through."

The darkness hid Gil Claggett's face. His sneer was audible. "The sheriff's looking for you, Daly. If you've dry-gulched Yance, it'll be something else to answer for."

Sundown took Gil Claggett's gun and thrust it behind his belt. He holstered his own gun. "Let's go, Gil."

Gil Claggett swung on him with the speed of a striking snake. A fist caught Sundown on the cheek. His left hand grabbed Sundown's gun wrist, blocking the draw. As Sundown staggered, Gil snatched for the gun behind Sundown's belt.

He was as big as Sundown, quicker, if anything. A shot would bring men running. Sundown thought of that as he reeled from the blow. Then, throwing himself forward against Gil Claggett, he got at his left gun and drew it. The barrel swung up against Gil Claggett's head with a dull impact.

Claggett suddenly went limp and staggered against the house. He would have fallen if Sundown had not held him up. It was some moments before he was himself.

"Ought to have shot you then," Sundown said through his teeth. "Next time you'll get it."

Gil Claggett went with him without further protest. Sundown led the black behind them as they walked down the street. Fifty yards off they met Claggett's Mexican. He peered at them, hesitated as if waiting for an order. Gil Claggett ignored him. The Mexican went on toward the house.

A light was burning in the sheriff's office next to the jail. Sundown left the horse at the hitch rack in front and took Gil Claggett to the door. Wallace was at a desk at the side of the room, smoking a cigarette, writing busily. A prodding gun muzzle sent Gil Claggett in ahead of Sundown.

Wallace looked up, came quickly to his feet, reaching for the gun belt lying on top of his desk.

"Steady, Sheriff," Sundown warned.

Wallace dropped his hand, facing them. The cigarette was steady as it raised to his lips.

"Might have expected something like this, Daly. What's the matter with your head, Claggett? It's bleeding."

In the light Gil Claggett looked much younger than his brother, but as big and good-looking. He burst out violently: "He trapped me on my porch and bent a gun barrel over my head! And brought me here! What are you going to do about it?"

Wallace smiled thinly under his black mustache. "Not

much right now, with a gun in my face. I'm no fool. Daly, what's on your mind? I've been looking for you."

"I heard," Sundown agreed. "You and Claggett sit in them chairs against the opposite wall where you won't be tempted to start anything."

He reached back without taking his eyes off the two men, pulled the curtain on the door, and slipped the heavy bolt, then moved over a step and did the same to the window shade.

The sheriff and Claggett had dropped down in the chairs. Wallace was gnawing the end of his black mustache now and frowning. He said curtly as Sundown walked to the door at the rear of the room and bolted it: "This has gone about far enough, Daly. I don't like to be held up in my own jail."

"Too bad we don't get everything we like," Sundown said. "I didn't like to be blamed for holding up that Paradise stage. Might have done it, if I needed the money, but I just happened by in time to get the blame. If anybody'd taken time to look back on my trail, they've seen where I was riding alone all day. Those jaspers didn't give me time to say it."

"Lie down with the hogs and you get up with mud," Wallace said bluntly. "You aimed to run with the McKays, and that gets you all the dirt in the territory. The sheriff over Paradise way read your sign next morning and sent out word you might not be the man they wanted, after all. I'm ready to forget it. But I want you for killing a Wagon Wheel man on Cowpen Creek. That crooked hind shoe on your horse is a dead giveaway."

"And he had the nerve to threaten *me!*" Gil Claggett snorted.

"Shut up," Sundown said. "The McKays shot that Wagon Wheel man, Sheriff. I just happened to be there. They plugged him in the back after he busted into a little play they were making. Rex McKay and a cold-eyed little gun shark by the name of Salty O'Shea dropped him with their rifles."

Wallace raised his cigarette deliberately, inhaled, and let smoke dribble up through his black mustache. "That so? You just happened to be around when trouble busts, don't you?"

Gil Claggett sneered. "It's always a good idea to blame everything on the McKays."

Sundown fixed him with a cold eye. "Mebbeso, at that, since you an' your brother are runnin' with the McKays. An' the sheriff, too."

"What's that?" Wallace slammed his cigarette to the floor and came out of his chair. "Damn you, Daly, what do you mean by that?'

"You heard me, Wallace. I said you were running with the McKays, too. Calm down."

A startled look flashed over Gil Claggett's face—apprehension, uneasiness—but as Wallace sank back in the chair angrily, Gil Claggett shrugged. "He's crazy as a locoed steer, Wallace."

"I believe it," Wallace agreed violently.

"Mebbe you can explain them Double Anchor yearlings the McKays threw over on Wagon Wheel land the other day," Sundown said mildly. "Somebody's taken a running iron an' blotted 'em over into Wagon Wheels."

"You're lying!" Wallace said savagely. "None of my cattle has been rebranded this year! And none of them has been thrown over on Enoch Lee's range!"

Sundown said dreamily: "I saw the McKays drive 'em on Enoch Lee's land. I saw the blotted brands. Dan Steele busted into it an' got shot in the back. I heard Yance Claggett go over the deal with Jupiter McKay this morning. You're mixed up in it, too."

"The hell I am!" Wallace shouted, pounding the arm of his

chair. "If any man said so, he lied!"

"And so," Sundown said in the same dreamy tone, "seeing Enoch Lee was gettin' knifed in the back by his friend Yance, and my number was up as soon as Jupiter McKay got around to obligin' Claggett, I appointed myself unofficial deputy of the county. You're hereby relieved from office, Wallace, and as acting-deputy I'll ride herd on the job. First, we'll throw Gil in a cell where he can't leak out. An' then we'll round up a posse and go lookin' for trouble."

"I told you he was crazy!" Gil Claggett snarled.

"Gil, where's Yance?" Wallace asked suddenly.

"Saw him this afternoon," Gil lied glibly. "He dropped in at the house for a minute, an' then rode out again."

Sundown sighed. "When you lie like that, Gil, it makes me envious. I tried to be a skunk, too, but I can't stand the stink. Git back in your cell, and, if I hear one yip out of you, I'm comin' in an' pistol-whip a new face on you. Wallace, put him in."

Wallace looked at the pistol, and stood up obediently. "Sorry, Gil," he said. "Looks like there's nothing else to do."

"You're not going to lock me up!" Gil Claggett said furiously.

"Git!" said Sundown. "Peaceable, too. I been waiting two years to get at you. I'm fightin' temptation now."

Muttering under his breath, Gil Claggett walked back into the small cell-block. He was the only prisoner. Wallace locked him in and returned to the office silently. Sundown ejected the shells from the sheriff's gun, emptied the belt loops, and held the useless gear out.

"Wear it, so you'll look regular," he directed. "Now make me a real deputy with a deputy's badge."

Wallace took a nickel badge from a desk drawer. "I'd better swear you in," he suggested.

"Shoot."

It took but a moment. Sundown grinned wryly. "I've come a long way since they let me out of the pen. Now pay attention, Wallace. I want a posse. You give the orders." Sundown holstered his gun. "I'll be at your elbow. Don't get careless. I want all the men you can raise in a half an hour. We're riding to Enoch Lee's first."

"And then?" Wallace asked with an expressionless face.

"We'll see," said Sundown. "I'm gamblin' on what a couple of crooks will do. Bein' crooked, they ought to think just one way."

"I'll have to know what the posse's riding into," Wallace said stubbornly. "There'll be married men in it. Friends of mine. I'll lead them into no trap, Daly."

They faced one another, equally big and broad-shouldered. Wallace, gray-haired and rock-like in his responsibility and resolve. Sundown, lean, hard, muscular, younger but equally as hard-faced. The clash of wills struck tension in the small office.

"You said you were going to clean the McKays out before you left office," Sundown said abruptly. "You're doing it tonight, Wallace. They've been hiding out at the old Death's Head Mine. Yance Claggett is workin' with them. I left him tied up back in the foothills. I'm out to bust him and the McKays tonight."

"I'll not lead a posse up to Death's Head Mine tonight," Wallace said flatly. "I know the place. You have to go through a trap to get to the mine. Half a dozen men could hold it."

"Not even to prove you ain't feeding at the same trough with the McKays?"

Wallace's face grew bleak, angry. "What are you driving at, Daly?'

"Skunks," said Sundown laconically. "Couldn't stand them in the pen and I can't now. That takes in the Claggetts, the McKays, and this Wagon Wheel deal."

Wallace nodded, reached for his Stetson. "Let's get the posse together," he said briefly.

VIII

"DEATH AT THE WAGON WHEEL"

They rode out of Las Piedras an hour later, the clash of hoofs on the rocky ground striking against the night as they topped the mesa and rode southeast toward the Wagon Wheel range and the mountains beyond.

Wallace rode at the head, Sundown beside him. Eleven armed men followed—all the good riders that Wallace had been able to gather without turning to the ranchers. Wallace's gun was still empty; he carried a rifle, but had no cartridges for it.

Sundown had been standing beside him, grimly silent, in those moments in front of the jail when Wallace had told the men they were riding out after the McKays who had killed Dan Steele on Cowpen Creek.

"Enoch Lee will have his men ready," Wallace had told them bluntly. "I'm leaving Harvey Greer behind to round up more men. The McKays are hiding out at the Death's Head Mine up north of Surprise Cañon on Boulder Mountain. They've killed one man. They rustled a lot of my beef, and they're evidently set to raise hell on Las Piedras range for some time. If we meet 'em, there'll be gun talk. Any man who hasn't the guts for it better drop out now."

That was what Sundown had told Wallace to say. Wallace himself had towered before the men sternly. No one had dropped out.

There were men among the eleven who recognized Sundown. Several who had been his friends greeted him cordially. All had noticed the deputy's badge on his shirt. They were curious. They discussed it in asides among themselves, but no man questioned his right to be at Wallace's elbow, apparently by Wallace's wish.

Wallace spoke out of the corner of his mouth as they rode. "This is a queer play, Daly. I haven't forgotten you set out to join the McKays. If this is a double-cross and we're trapped, I'll hunt you down myself!"

"Gracias," Sundown said. "Wallace, I'll have the whole Las Piedras range yappin' at my heels if this keeps on. I'll give you fair warning . . . look for trouble anytime. Pull up your posse somewhere along here and I'll tell you what to do."

Wallace stopped his men after the next quarter of a mile. A low-voiced request took him off a hundred yards with Sundown.

"We'll cut the Wagon Wheel house road just ahead," said Sundown. "Tell your men to drop back a mile or so, and follow us easy. You and I'll sashay on alone."

"It doesn't make sense," Wallace objected irritably. "What are you up to?"

"I'm gamblin' that a smart crook always overreaches himself. That's why they get hung or land in the pen so often."

"Meaning me?"

"Meaning everybody connected with this Wagon Wheel deal, Wallace. Tell 'em."

Wallace reined back to his men and gave his orders curtly. Then the sheriff and Sundown rode on ahead alone.

Sundown passed his sombrero over to Wallace as they went. "There's a double handful of cartridges in it, Wallace."

Wallace passed the hat back, empty, a few moments later. "Nothing to stop me from taking you in now, Daly."

"Nope," Sundown agreed. "Why don't you?"

"I want to see what you're up to."

"You will," Sundown promised.

His words were prophecy. They rode a mile farther, topped the rise on the narrow dirt track they were following, and the Wagon Wheel lights were in the near distance. A horse nickered at the side of the road. The stir of riders off in the dark paralleled their course.

A voice called: "That you, Daly?"

Sundown drew his gun in the darkness and called back: "It's me. Who is it?"

A second voice, close by, laughed shrilly: "It's me, Daly! Jupiter McKay! We been waitin' for you!"

Wallace uttered a round oath furiously. "I was looking for something like this, Daly! By God, I'll kill you first!"

"Damn you, ride for the ranch house!" said Sundown. "An' argue later!" His gun blast laced the night with orange fire in the direction of Jupiter McKay's voice. He deeply drove the spurs. The black leaped forward.

The night was thick about them, hiding the men offside the road. Jupiter McKay shouted: "Gil Claggett, drop back an' we'll get him!"

Close on the heels of that the drum of quick pursuit was drowned in the clash and roar of gunfire. Bending low in the saddle, Sundown heard the vicious whine of lead lacing the darkness about him.

They had been lined up alongside the road, the whole McKay gang it seemed. They rode a gauntlet, a gauntlet of death, and only the quickness of their getaway and the darkness saved him. Sundown emptied his belt gun and reloaded as he rode. Wallace swept up beside him, firing as he came. No words were spoken, but the suspicion and distrust that had been between them was no more.

The gunfire behind them slacked off. Later Sundown was to know that the McKays had been confused by Gil Claggett's failure to join them. They had received strict orders that no harm must come to him. In the darkness Jupiter McKay had mistaken the sheriff for Gil Claggett.

The pursuit swept down the long slope after them, and the lights of the Wagon Wheel ranch house quickly drew near. The McKays were dropping farther and farther behind, although, seeming in no hurry to close up against the flaming guns, they followed. That, too, was quickly explained.

Spurring, slashing hard, they swept up to the ranch house, standing silently, quietly. The front door was closed. The windows were shut. No horses or men were in evidence, only the barking dogs that warily kept their distance as they clamored.

"Something's wrong!" Sundown yelled to Wallace as they rode up.

"What?" Wallace queried.

Sundown reined sharply before the *portal,* struck the ground running, and made for the front door.

"Who's that?" a sharp, familiar voice demanded out of the darkness.

"Daly!" Sundown panted mechanically. "Where is everybody?"

"Where they won't do any good, you damn' meddler!" the voice snarled.

Sundown dodged, grabbing for his gun, as he recognized the speaker. It was Rex McKay!

Surprise—absolute, complete. Orange flame and the roar of a shot drove aside the *portal* shadows the next instant. Sundown spun half around as a hammer blow struck his shoulder. The shock dazed him. He knew he was badly hit, and for fatal seconds his body refused to function as he staggered and almost went down. His whole left side had been numbed by the impact of the heavy lead slug.

Two paces away a split instant later Wallace's gun thundered, a brace of shots sounding at once. The dull thud of Rex McKay's dropping revolver was audible. His strangled gasp was barely understandable.

"Claggett . . . don't you know me? It's Rex McKay! You . . . you shot the wrong man!"

"I don't reckon so," Wallace said harshly.

He was not answered. Rex McKay groaned once, and then fell heavily.

"I got him!" Wallace said with satisfaction. He was now on the ground. "Daly, I apologize. Back there I had figured you'd led me right into a trap. I was set to plug you when you cut loose at the McKays. What's going on around here? Where's Enoch Lee and his men? Did McKay get you?" Wallace stepped close.

Sundown said through clenched teeth: "In the shoulder. Guess I'm all right. I can move my arm a little now. Something's wrong here, Wallace! Enoch Lee and his men should have been waiting! They'd've been out here now if they were here. Enoch Lee and Yance Claggett thought I was coming here this evening with Gil Claggett. Claggett told the McKays, like I figgered he would. I wonder what . . . what's inside the house?"

The door opened abruptly as Sundown finished in a swift rush of words. A small, slender, stoop-shouldered figure stepped out, peering. The tangle of uncut hair under his worn Stetson was silhouetted against the light that struck through the doorway. His gliding progress, gun in hand, his wizened mask of a face stamped him for what he was—a killer.

"Get him all right, Rex?" he asked with no concern in his voice.

"Too bad, Salty!" Sundown said softly. "Drop your gun an' reach high!"

The McKays were coming up with a rush as Sundown spoke. The action at the *portal* had flashed by in a few brief moments. Salty O'Shea moved with the speed of a striking rattler, snapping his gun toward the direction of Sundown's voice before his body turned.

Sundown, a scant two paces away, was in action at the first move. His gun swung up, dropped down, and smashed Salty O'Shea's gun wrist with a terrific blow as it came around. Cursing with pain, the little man grabbed at a broken wrist as the gun fell from his helpless fingers. He tried to dodge. Sundown tripped him.

"Get him, Wallace!" Sundown bit out. "Take him in the house! They'll corner us here on the *portal* in a minute!"

Wallace pounced on the scrambling, cursing figure of Salty O'Shea, and jerked the little man roughly upright. Gripping O'Shea behind the neck, he booted him through the doorway. Sundown caught up the fallen gun and followed hastily as the drumming rush of the McKays pounded up to the house. A stout wooden bar stood in the corner beside the door. Sundown dropped it into heavy brackets as men dismounted and hurried to the *portal*. He paused a moment, listening.

Jupiter McKay's high shrill voice said excitedly: "They ain't here! That must 'a' been them went in the house! What's the matter? Rex didn't get him? There was shootin'!"

"Mebbe Rex dropped him an' took Claggett inside," another voice suggested. "Strike a match, somebody!"

A moment later there were exclamations, oaths. Jupiter McKay's shrill voice rose in a fury of grief. "*It's Rex!* He's dead! Daly killed him!"

"That Daly," one of the men said violently, "must wear a

horseshoe around his neck and a rabbit's foot in his pocket. He's hell for luck, an' a shootin' fool!"

Jupiter McKay raved: "He's in there! Get him out! I'll tear his heart out with my own hands! I'll drag him from here to the mine on my own rope! Break in the door!"

Sundown flattened himself against the wall and called: "You old buzzard, it ain't healthy in here! That worthless whelp of yours didn't get all the hell that's loose tonight!"

"Get 'em!" Jupiter McKay yelled.

Guns barked on the other side of the door. Lead ripped and poured through the planks. Sundown shot back twice through the door. For a moment the shooting ceased. He seized the instant of peace to slide along the wall to the door of the living room. As he stepped through, they opened up on the door from an angle.

Yance Claggett had been standing in the living room with his arm about Jordan Lee's shoulder when Wallace entered with his prisoner. Yance Claggett was staring at Wallace as if seeing a ghost.

"I thought it was Gil coming in," he said in a queer voice as Sundown stepped into the room.

Wallace took a tighter grip on his squirming, cursing prisoner, and lightly cuffed him with the barrel of his revolver. The sheriff's voice was expressionless as he spoke to Yance Claggett. "You thought it was Gil, Yance. Why?"

"Why . . . why, Daly said he was going to bring Gil back," Yance stammered.

"And that's why these McKay gunmen were waiting at the front door?" Wallace questioned.

Jordan Lee slipped out of Claggett's arm. Her face was pale, her eyes big. But in that moment, before she spoke, Sundown got again a feeling of a river rising behind barriers, ready to burst.

"McKay gunmen?" she said to Wallace in a tight voice. "You must be mistaken. They were waiting to see my father about some cattle. Yance knew them. We've been talking to them in here."

"I never saw them before, Jordan!" Claggett denied harshly. "You were mistaken!"

Salty O'Shea, gibbering with pain and helpless anger, snarled: "Damn you Claggett! You don't walk out on me like this! If you had any guts, you'd've been out there with a gun, backin' me up! You said Daly was coming back with your brother. An' he brought the sheriff! I think you double-crossed us. Daly, I wish I'd've shot you back there on Cowpen Creek the other day!"

Yance Claggett looked like a drowning man, snatching at straws. "Wallace," he said hoarsely, "the man's lying! He doesn't know what he's saying! I'm a deputy! I'm with you on this! Let me have him an' I'll lock him up while you hold those gunmen off outside. Where's Gil? Why didn't you bring him? He's a deputy, too."

"Gil had his eye teeth pulled," Sundown drawled. "He's locked in a cell back in Las Piedras."

"That right, Wallace?" Yance Claggett asked gruffly.

Wallace nodded. "That's right, Yance. And it looks to me like you're going to join him. Miss Lee, where's your father?"

The firing outside had ceased. Curtains had been drawn over the living room windows, shutting off the gaze of anyone outside. While Sundown stepped swiftly over to them and listened, Jordan Lee answered Wallace.

"Dad took his men and rode to Las Piedras to find you, Sheriff. They took the short cut. They must have missed you." She swung on Yance Claggett. "*You* told Dad to go. You said you'd stay with me and see that everything was all right. And all the time you were working with the McKays!"

Yance Claggett winced at the blazing scorn in her voice. Then he whirled around, crouching, as a heavy crash sounded at the back of the house. They heard wood splintering, giving. . . .

IX

"FIRE!"

Sundown jumped for the open hall door, stopping just before he reached it. He heard Wallace cry out sharply: "Come back, Yance! Don't try it!"

There was a door near the great stone fireplace in the back wall of the room. Yance Claggett had leaped for it, was wrenching it open as Sundown looked over his shoulder. Wallace raised his gun, hesitated.

In that moment Yance Claggett whirled out of the room. But only for a moment. Loudly beyond the door a gun exploded twice. Claggett cried out, staggering back against the door, then reeled back into the room.

Jordan Lee cried out, too, involuntarily, as she saw his face. A bullet had struck him below the eyes. For one awful instant the bulging eyes, in that face that had once been so handsome, looked at them glassily. They were the eyes of a dead man who still moved. Yance Claggett's mouth opened, emitted a hoarse, unnatural croak, wondering, dazed.

"They shot me!" Yance Claggett got out. His bandaged right hand lifted jerkily toward his face—and never reached it. Yance Claggett fell there in the doorway, and no one could have helped him if there had been time.

From the next room a yell came. "That was Claggett, Jim! You plugged him!"

"Hell!" said Jim. "I thought it was Daly! Why didn't he yell?"

Wallace was at the doorway by then, pumping shots through it across Yance Claggett's body. He was answered only once, and the bullet knocked splinters from the door edge by his shoulder. A door at the back of the next room slammed heavily.

Wallace hauled Yance Claggett's still form aside and closed the door, saying disgustedly: "They wouldn't shoot it out."

Salty O'Shea had been left standing helplessly in the middle of the floor. He ducked as a gun spoke out in front, and glass crashed, and a bullet smacked against the opposite wall. Beady-eyed, watchful, tense, he turned from Wallace to Sundown, scanning the room with the light of desperation in his eyes. Other shots came from the front, the bullets crashing through the windowpanes and smacking into the brick wall.

Ignoring them, Wallace walked to Salty O'Shea. His tanned, hard face showed no emotion as he said: "You're in the way here now. Can't bother with you." Wallace reached out a big hand, caught the smaller man to him, and calmly swung the barrel of his revolver behind Salty's ear. Salty went limp. Wallace let him drop, said simply: "He's dangerous."

Sundown grinned. "Mister, I take your dust for ever thinking you were hooked up with the McKays. Fact is, I never did really think you were, but I couldn't take any chances. You wouldn't have believed me, anyway, or brought a posse out here if I hadn't dealt the cards."

"Glad to see you're gettin' some sense," Wallace grunted. "Guess you're right at that. I'd have slapped you in a cell if I'd gotten to my gun first."

They could hear steps tramping at the back of the house, voices speaking, loud and unafraid. Jupiter McKay's shrill, bawling tones rose above all other sounds. "Get in the hall there! Block all the ways they can get out!"

Jordan Lee had been backed into the corner by Sundown. She had cried out involuntarily as Yance Claggett had reeled back into the room, then had stood silently. Now she reached to the corner behind her and caught up a light rifle, leaning there, and came toward the door where Sundown was standing. He swept her back with an arm.

"Get down where you'll be safe!" he rapped out. "This ain't your game!"

She knocked his arm away. Her dark eyes were blazing. Her brown hair hardly came to Sundown's shoulder. But she became more than a slip of a girl as she answered him, more than the slender little beauty he had first seen. Once more her young face was oddly mature, tense, stubborn, angry. "They're in my house!" she declared. "They've come to kill! Do you think I'll stand helplessly by like . . . like a silly child while they do this?"

Standing there with his blood-soaked shoulder and the pain stabbing him with every movement, Sundown grinned at her. It was like a fragment out of a dream. Men tramping and shouting at the back of the house, shots crashing through the windowpanes and raking the room, death all about the house, closing in on them—and yet for a few moments they seemed apart from all of this, alone.

"You win," he said, and Sundown didn't realize then how gentle his voice was for the first time. Jordan Lee did. "I guess maybe we'll need you, after all, before this is over," he said, and whirled to the door as feet rushed along the hall. A man, two men, guns held ready, appeared.

Gun steadied across his forearm, Sundown shot deliberately in a tearing crescendo. The first man plunged to the floor. The second dodged back out of sight, then caught an ankle of the fallen man and dragged him back, too.

Powder smoke was drifting in hazy, acrid waves through the room. The air never seemed to lose the crashing reverberations of gunfire. Sundown moved back a step and awkwardly reloaded his gun, wincing as he had to move his left arm.

"Got him in the hollow!" Sundown said. "He'll be reformed from now on."

There was no cessation of the raking fire through the windows. But it was blind shooting, for the curtains still held up. A bullet smashed the lamp shade and chimney, and glass cascaded to the floor. Wallace crossed to the lamp and blew it out.

"Time that was done anyway," he said.

The half light in the hall, reflected from an open door in one of the rear rooms, was eerie, ghost-like. Jordan Lee's rifle barked suddenly at one of the front windows. She had crept there, lifted a corner of the curtain, and shot without warning.

"I think I hit him," she said calmly over her shoulder as she pumped a fresh shell into the breech. "I fired at the flash of his gun."

Jupiter McKay's shrill shout was clearly audible. "There's only two of them in there! Burn 'em out! Here's a can of coal oil!"

One of the men protested hoarsely: "Salty O'Shea's in there!"

"Damn Salty O'Shea! He had no business gettin' himself caught that way! If he'd been half the man I thought he was, my boy wouldn't be dead now!"

It was plain by Jupiter McKay's voice that the man was half mad with grief and fury.

Wallace showed emotion for the first time, and worry. "If they burn us out, we're done for," he said. "They've got the house surrounded. We haven't got a chance to fight out that way. I wonder where my men are?"

"We were a couple of miles ahead of them, travelin' fast," Sundown said. "We've only been here a few minutes."

"It seems like a longer time with all this hell bustin' loose," Wallace grunted in the darkness. His voice grew more worried than ever. "McKay has a lot of men out there. More than the eleven we brought. I don't know whether they can do much if they do come up. They're outnumbered. I hate to think of them walkin' into a thing like this an' gettin' shot to pieces." Even then, with death closing in inexorably, Wallace the peace officer was thinking of his men.

"Somebody has to get shot," Sundown said coolly, "an' you can't bust up the McKays by standin' off wondering what will happen. I figgered Enoch Lee an' his men would be here, waiting for us. But as long as old Jupiter McKay's hand is called, we might as well see how many cards he can lay on the line. We got to do one thing, though, Wallace. Get this girl out. They're a bad lot, but they won't hurt a woman. They've got no quarrel with her. Let's yell for a truce while she walks out."

"You will not!" Jordan said defiantly in the darkness. "I'm here, and here I'll stay! I wouldn't trust them, and I won't leave you two."

"I'd put her out," Sundown suggested through the darkness to Wallace, as he watched the faintly lighted doorway.

"Try it!" she flared.

She had hardly finished speaking when the hallway beyond Sundown glowed suddenly with the fierce red light of sweeping flames.

"Here we go!" said Sundown dryly. "Our own private little bonfire!"

The words were hardly out when there came a muffled

swish of flame. A cloud of fire and sparks sailed through the air and struck outside the door, flaring up wildly to the height of a man's shoulder. It was a bundle of blankets saturated with kerosene, burning more fiercely each instant. The red glare struck into the room. Heat followed. The choking smell of burning wood rolled over them.

Sundown kicked the door shut with his foot. "No use to drag it in and try to put it out," he commented calmly. "If I stick my nose out the door, I'll get it shot off."

"They've pitched one outside this door, too," Wallace said. "These pine doors will burn through in no time."

Sundown sighed. "It's as hard on them as us. The smoke goes both ways."

"We'll be burnt out like rats in a trap if we don't do something!" Wallace fumed.

"We'll get shot up with McKay lead if we bust out an' try to do something," Sundown retorted cheerfully. "We're damned if we do, and damned if we don't." He began to whistle softly through his teeth.

Wallace had judged the doors correctly. The dry, pitch-filled pine caught instantly. The panels cracked. Smoke began to seep through. The red glare glinted ominously through the cracks.

Jordan Lee moved close to Sundown, putting her hand on his arm. "It's going to be pretty bad," she said. "I'm not afraid, but . . . but I want to be near someone." Her voice was a bit unsteady, frightened.

Hearing it, Sundown felt red rage stirring for the first time. It swept away his cold bitterness. It made the thing personal, and in his throat, unspoken, he damned Jupiter McKay savagely. He holstered his gun and took her hand, her small, strong hand that had not been afraid of work. It lay coldly in his, then clung tightly, as if she found strength in the contact.

"Some way, somehow," said Sundown with a confidence he did not feel, "we'll get out of this. The McKay luck has held too long. It's due to bust tonight."

"I wish I thought so," she said uncertainly. Her fingers clung tighter in his.

Her heady presence was like wine—and there might be no tomorrow. Sundown swept her close, roughly, and kissed her with fierceness born of gunfire, of flame, and of death.

She gasped, and for a moment lay limply in his arms, against his chest. Her cheeks were satin smooth, her mouth soft, yielding. Then she was out of his arms, laughing in a choked rush.

"Sorry," Sundown muttered.

Her groping hand caught his again. It was no longer cold. "I'm not," said Jordan Lee. "I'm glad! I'll always be glad!"

"I'm a jailbird!" said Sundown hoarsely. "A no-account, worthless, low-down rannihan!"

"You are *you,*" she said.

She was like the river come to the sea, broad and deep as it met the tide and pushed to the deeper depths where there was peace.

Flying lead smashed through the windowpanes with vicious smacks. The crackling roar of flame eating through the doors rose higher. Glowing red spots drove back the blackness with a crimson glow. The heat was greater, the smoke thickening about them.

Wallace swore aloud. "I'll make a break for it before I roast in here!"

Sundown said to Jordan Lee: "The only way out is through these two doors?"

"Yes," she replied. "There used to be a door on the other

side of the fireplace, into a bedroom, but Dad made a storeroom out of it, and put a bookcase in the doorway and a closet on the other side."

Sundown touched her arm. "Come over to the bookcase. Duck low when you cross the room."

He went first. "Wallace," he said, "come here. I've got a surprise for you." Wallace joined him by the bookcase set into the wall, and filled solidly with volumes. "Let's throw the books on the floor!"

When that was done, Sundown ordered: "Take out the shelves." It was done. Boards were nailed across the back. "Kick them out at the bottom!" Sundown directed.

Wallace drove a boot through the bottom board; nails gave. In short seconds he had kicked two boards loose at one end. His powerful hands wrenched them free. There was room now to crawl through.

Sundown knelt at the opening, listened, heard nothing on the other side. He wriggled through, stood upright in a tangle of hanging clothes. He opened the door cautiously, peered into a black, silent, deserted room. "All right," he husked over his shoulder, and groped forward.

Boxes and trunks were stacked about. Shelves lined the walls. He found a single window, curtained. Wallace and Jordan Lee joined him there.

"Get her out!" Sundown urged Wallace. "They won't be watching this end of the house."

"You're coming, too?" she asked.

"Sure, I'll follow."

Wallace pushed the window up softly, climbed out, caught her in his arms as she followed. Sundown heard the soft patter of their steps for an instant—and then they were gone in the night.

A man came running from the front of the house. Sundown's gun slid over the window sill. But the fellow passed, unseeing, to the rear.

The high-pitched voice of Jupiter McKay sounded back inside the house. Sundown turned and crossed the room. He found a door in the corner. It was unlocked, the key on the inside. He opened the door cautiously.

A blast of heat and the smoke struck him in the face. The red glare of fire enveloped him.

The room was empty. Fire blazed furiously about the door at the front of the room. At the back a door stood ajar, and it was through there the voice of Jupiter McKay was coming. It sounded as if McKay were just outside the door.

Sundown gulped a deep breath, hunched his shoulders, and plunged into the heat and smoke. Face set grimly, gun steady in hand. He reached the door, kicked it open with his foot. Jupiter McKay was standing a scant arm's length away, his back to the door.

On sudden impulse Sundown jammed his gun in the holster, reached out. Jupiter McKay felt his presence, or felt the sudden wave of heat. He started to turn. Sundown's big hand clamped on the back of the outlaw leader's neck at the same instant. With a mighty yank he brought McKay through the door and spun him back into the room.

McKay struck a chair, half fell, and came up with the quickness of a cat, whirling around to the door on his bandy legs. He saw Sundown, and venom and fury boiled across his face. In that moment his spindle-shanked, slightly grotesque figure, with its pink cheeks and coarse red eyebrows, looked like something monstrous. A thin, high-pitched cry of fury burst from him.

They faced each other through the roiling smoke. Between them tension hung at the snapping point.

Sundown held his good hand breast high. His face was a

grim mask. "Here I am, you double-crossin' old wolf!" he said. "You wanted me, an' now you got me. Go for your gun, McKay! You got a chance!"

X

"THE LAST OF THE RED MCKAYS"

Jupiter McKay's tight-lipped mouth went to a slit. He hesitated, his cold eyes wavering. Then one lean, powerful hand flashed to the gun at his hip.

He was fast, a dead shot, and starting on even terms. But that taut, raised hand of Sundown's dropped like a passing shadow. His gun leaped from the holster like a thing alive. He shot while the muzzle of Jupiter McKay's gun was still lifting.

The monstrous, bandy-legged figure reeled forward through the smoke. The gun exploded into the floor. An instant later Jupiter McKay pitched forward, face down, gun flying from his fingers.

Coughing, choking from the smoke, Sundown stepped to him, caught a leg, and dragged the prone figure into the storeroom. He was not an instant too soon. Men boiled through the doorway from the hall as he straightened up. A yell announced that he was seen. A gun jerked in his direction.

Sundown fired a snap shot from his hip, leaped aside as a second shot answered. He felt the bullet tear the hair vest, and then the wall hid him. They would have to come through the door to get him. Sundown waited grimly, wiping the back of his hand across his watering eyes. The smoke was fast filling the storeroom, too.

In that moment the thunder of drumming hoofs drifted through the open window. Men whooped loudly. The sharp crackle of gunfire burst out all around the house.

"Trouble, boys! Everyone outside! Get the horses! McKay's dead! It's every man for himself!"

Sundown reloaded his gun and followed them. Not a McKay man was in sight as he entered the back hall. Outside the shots and yells continued. Men cried out with pain, with unintelligible orders, and requests. Horses galloped off furiously.

No need to wonder what had happened. Wallace's posse had swept down in belated but startling surprise. Without a leader the McKays scattered like chaff before a wind. Through the back door, as Sundown reached it, burst the stubby, bearded figure of Enoch Lee, brandishing a revolver. Recognizing Sundown, he shouted hoarsely: "Where's my daughter?"

"Outside. Safe," Sundown told him. "I thought you were Wallace's posse."

Enoch Lee raised a shaking hand and pushed his hat onto the back of his head. No longer was he the stern, ascetic, righteously hard man. Fear had broken through his shell of reserve.

"We followed the posse from Las Piedras," he said unsteadily. "Caught up with them on the road, talked a few minutes, and then took our time following Wallace. Are you sure Jordan is all right?"

"Wallace got her out of here a few minutes ago. As soon as the McKays are on the run, get some men in here to put these fires out."

The McKays were already on the run; some were shot down as they ran from the house, others scattered into the night afoot, and a few on horseback. The shooting stopped almost as quickly as it started. Enoch Lee shouted orders, sending men into the house to attack the flames.

Wallace came out of the night with Jordan Lee. Later, when the fire had been beaten down with blankets and killed with buckets of water, and the wounded and dead were being collected by the posse and the Wagon Wheel men, Enoch Lee faced Wallace, Jordan, and Sundown. From them he heard what had happened during his absence. He was a sobered man, Enoch Lee. "I didn't believe the McKays would come to the Wagon Wheel tonight," he confessed. "I wanted to see you about those blotted brands, Wallace."

Wallace shrugged. "It was no doing of mine. I've questioned a couple of the McKay men we've got tied up. The McKays rustled them off my land. They wanted your land. You wouldn't sell. The Claggetts, who have been working with them for years, buying rustled cattle, lent you money so they could foreclose. The Wagon Wheel is a natural entrance to Surprise Cañon and then through the mountains. It was a smooth deal to get you out of the way without violence. But thanks to Daly, here, it misfired. He saved you tonight, Enoch Lee, although I'm not clear yet how he knew what he was doing."

Sundown grinned sheepishly. "The McKays were after me. I tied Claggett up in the hills and ran his horse off, but fixed it so he could get loose, figgerin' he'd walk in to the ranch here, or run across the McKays and tell 'em I was going to bring his brother out to the ranch tonight and tip their hand. If they went to town tryin' to catch us, they might miss us. All they had to do was wait around the ranch and jump us when we showed up. I figgered you'd be here with your men, armed and ready, Mister Lee. Wallace and I left the posse back a ways and came on alone, like I was bringin' Gil Claggett. I figgered they'd jump us, and we'd have the McKays caught between the posse and the men here at the ranch." Sundown shrugged. "I didn't figger on your being away."

Enoch Lee fingered his beard. "It seems I was a rash and headstrong man," he admitted. "I distrusted you, Daly. I thought harshly of you. But I'll make amends. There's a place here for you at the ranch, if you'll take it."

"No," said Wallace. "I made him a deputy. I like his style. I'll keep him. We'll keep the McKays on the run until they're all cleared out."

Jordan Lee spoke then, with the calmness of certainty. "First you'll be a deputy, and then a cowman. Time for both."

Sundown grinned. "The ayes have it. But there's one thing that can't wait. I'll settle that while my shoulder's being bandaged."

"What's he talkin' about," Enoch Lee demanded with some asperity, when he and the sheriff were alone a moment later. "And why's she holdin' him up with her arm around his waist? He can walk all right."

Wallace grinned. "He's a man from boots to hair," he said. "I reckon he'll settle everything all right. Reckon, too, he's a little weak right now, while he leads up to it."

A Stranger Rides

T. T. Flynn completed "A Stranger Rides" on March 14, 1932. As written, it ran forty-three typescript pages. Marguerite E. Harper, T. T. Flynn's agent, sent it to Rogers Terrill at Popular Publications. Terrill asked that the story be cut for reasons of space to accommodate other stories (the first two issues of *Dime Western*, 12/32 and 1/33, would both be carrying Flynn stories). Once the story was cut, it appeared in the third issue of *Dime Western* (2/33) under the title "Reward Hungry." In the event of their publication, Flynn's stories in the first two issues proved so popular with readers that never again would he be asked to cut any story he submitted. The author did not retain his original typescript (possibly it was destroyed in the revision process), so for its first book appearance only the title of this story could be restored.

Three horsemen met at the forks, where the Torques trail joined the Valley trail and, falling in together, jogged toward the town of Huachaca. Two of them had come thirty miles that day through Torques Pass—Monte Davis, slim, level-eyed, and thoughtful, and Chris Temple, younger and shorter, stockier. They were from Rabbit Flats, and owned the Rabbit Ear brand between them.

The third rider was Johnny Simpson from Wonder Wells, his face long, easy, good-natured. Johnny had been married a short two months.

Monte lounged sideways in the saddle, hands resting easily on the saddle horn, and surveyed Johnny with approval as they rode. Two months of marriage had done wonders, Monte reflected. Johnny had been a hard worker, a good friend, but silent, taciturn, almost morose at times. Now he was smiling, alert, breaking into snatches of song.

Johnny pulled out his belt gun, fired once, off the trail. A brown nest of taut coils flowed out into aimless writhings.

"Got him!" Johnny exclaimed cheerfully. "I swear I never seen so many rattlers any year. I'm shot out. Only one cartridge left." He slipped a finger over the empty loops of his belt and began to whistle softly through his teeth.

"Lend you some," Chris offered.

"Thanks . . . no. I'll stock up in the morning before I start back."

The late afternoon sun was still hot over jagged Paloduro Peaks, when they rode into Huachaca, where cottonwoods and willows raised a shield of cool green on the dry buff slopes, and a gaunt black water tank marked the steel thread of the railroad. Crosby, the sheriff, stepped out from the sidewalk before his office and stopped them.

"Park your belt guns here, boys," he said curtly. "Them's the rules now."

Monte surveyed the sheriff without favor. He had never liked Crosby, tall, broad-shouldered, and gruff behind a heavy black mustache that straggled over his surly mouth. He had heard of Crosby's ruling and was of half a mind now to dispute it, but none of them was a troublemaker.

But Johnny Simpson laughed, unbuckled his belt, and handed it over. Monte shrugged and followed suit, and Chris did the same.

Monte watched Crosby head into his office. "I respect a dog," he said irrelevantly. "It knows when to bristle." He rode on to the Atlantic House, whose upper balcony and lower porch dominated Huachaca.

"Side me to the bar, boys. I'm buying," Chris said as they dismounted.

Johnny Simpson smiled sheepishly. "I'm a married man now. I promised Mary. . . ."

"Go with Cupid," Chris mourned. "And if you give out, come back. I'll buy."

But Johnny did not come back.

Shortly after Monte and Chris had taken their horses to the livery stable, a series of shrill blasts drew them to the small, frame station where they watched the accommodation train roll in for its brief, daily stop. A short wiry passenger, carrying a battered straw suitcase, alighted and approached them, smiling apologetically below the stiff black hat perched awkwardly on his head.

"How do I get to the sheriff's office?" he inquired.

"Up the street on the right," Monte directed. "You'll see his office just beyond the hardware store."

The stranger thanked him and walked off, straw suitcase bumping his leg.

Chris gazed reflectively after him. "Just like sending a lamb into a lobo's den. Wonder how much of his hide Crosby'll get."

"He packs a steely eye," Monte mused. "Crosby's a crook, but don't call your shots too early. I kinda fancy the little feller."

Later that evening, after dinner, they found the stranger drinking lemonade in the Atlantic bar. " 'Evening," he greeted jovially. "Have a drop with me."

"Lemonade," Chris accepted, rolling a warning eye at the

bartender's unbelieving stare.

"Me, too." Monte grinned. "And no sugar in Chris's, Charley. He's too sweet now. Friend, I'm Monte Davis and this is my partner, Chris Temple."

"Glad to know you both," beamed the stranger. "My name is Jonathan Morely. From Ashton, Ohio. Sheriff there. I've been admiring your town."

"It's got law an' order," said Chris. "*Muy, sí.* What kind of a town is your Ashton, Ohio, mister?"

Monte smiled behind his drink as he saw civic pride brighten Morely's face. Chris, he judged, had tapped a subject dear to Morely's heart, and he was right.

"Ashton is one of the coming centers of the state, sir. Fifty years from now she will be the queen of the packet-boat ports."

Morely brought out a large leather wallet and took from it a sheaf of papers. As he leafed through them, a small picture slipped out and fell to the floor. Monte returned it. Morely's gaze swept him sharply, then relaxed as he saw Monte was not interested.

"This is our waterfront," he said proudly, showing them another picture.

"Mmm-mm," Chris murmured politely. "Nothing like that around here. If one of them big white boats ever came crawlin' up the Río Grande, it'd scare every jack rabbit white an' reform the burros."

Monte admired the picture, too, and, without Morely knowing it, studied the man closely. His first impression was borne out. Morely, for all his Eastern ways, was nobody's fool. His face was stamped with lines of experience. There was a grim tilt to his jaw. He looked hard, wiry, fit in body and mind. He could be a dangerous man. In a few minutes Monte made an excuse and left with Chris.

Outside Monte said slowly: "That picture I picked up off the floor looked mighty like Johnny Simpson before sin got him and Mary rescued him."

Chris scoffed: "What'd Morely be doing with Johnny's picture?"

Monte held up five fingers, doubled them down one by one as he spoke. Morely's a sheriff. Comes from back East. Johnny did, too, one time. Morley went straight to Crosby's office. He read my face mighty sharp when I picked up that picture." Monte balled the doubled fingers into a fist. "Five parts down an' they make a whole."

"A whole what?"

"That's Johnny's call. We better tell him."

"I reckon so," Chris agreed. "He said he was going over to Jim Clancy's house for supper. He was hitched there, you know."

Jim Clancy's house, a one-story adobe behind two giant cottonwoods, was a stone's throw off Gila Street. Monte knocked. Jim Clancy answered.

"Johnny here?" Monte asked.

"Sure. Come in, boys."

"Thanks, Jim. Can't wait. Ask Johnny to step out."

Johnny came, grinning. "Come in," he urged. "I was just making out an order for some Chicago clothes from Missus Clancy's catalogue. Surprise for Mary."

"Can't now," Monte refused. "Just saw something funny over at the Atlantic House. Sheriff from Ashton, Ohio, was drinkin' with us. He dropped a picture that looked mighty familiar."

In the silence that followed Monte watched Johnny's joyousness fall away, and the impulse that had brought him here hardened into determination. Johnny might have a past. Who didn't in this new country? But he had earned a new deal in Huachaca—a deal he would not get from Crosby. Johnny's face was bleak and expressionless, his nostrils tensed, drawn, as he searched their faces.

"Chris and me are both believers in friends," Monte said gently. "They understand better, and most times are glad to help."

Johnny reached back and closed the door. His voice held grief. "This will be hard on Mary."

"As bad as that?"

"Yes. I've been hoping I'd outrun it. I'll tell you."

"Don't bother. Most of us look back on mistakes. Our spread's a good place to lay up. There's a bunk there for you, and a remuda of horses for your pick."

Johnny's hand, groping in the dark, caught Monte's in a mighty grip. "My friends!" Johnny said huskily. That was all; it was enough.

"Two thousand is the reward," continued Johnny swiftly. "Embezzlement. But I didn't do it. When they swore out a warrant, I got away. Drifted out here, started over under another name. They've traced me some way. Letters, I guess."

"Get a fresh horse at the livery stable an' fog it to your own place at Wonder Wells tonight," Chris suggested. "Tomorrow you can drift on over to Rabbit Flats. Monte an' me'll come in with news. Best not go back to the hotel. The sheriff is hanging around there."

"Nothing in my room. Was going to buy in the morning." Johnny's voice went bitter. "I'll not be dragged back an' lawed for something I didn't do! I'm young! Mary's young! I'll fight first!"

"Get out to Mary," Monte directed. "Tell her. She has a right to know. Her kind understands. We'll see you tomorrow."

"Soon as I tell the Clancys good bye, I'll leave," Johnny promised.

Monte felt better as they walked away, but he was still troubled. He had the feeling that something was eluding him. Just what he couldn't say. Crosby knew Johnny was in town. Morely must have shown him the picture, told what he was after, named the reward. Why wasn't Johnny under arrest already? Crosby was no friend of Johnny's. Inability to find the answer left Monte uneasy.

"We are fixin' to cheat the law, an' I'm proud of it," Chris said. "Statute books don't seem to stack so high against two like Johnny and Mary."

"That's right," Monte agreed. But he still remained uneasy. The feeling was still there hours later when there was no doubt that Johnny was safely out of town, far on his way to Wonder Wells.

"Think I'll look Morely up an' cultivate him some more," Monte decided finally. "I'll be a bald head to a bull pup there's a rannihan in the woodpile about this business."

The clerk at the Atlantic House informed them that Morely was not in, had said he might be gone all night.

"If that little feller has followed Johnny outta town, there's gonna be hell an' high water," Chris said under his breath as they walked away.

"He had to hire a hoss if he went. Let's check the livery stable," said Monte thoughtfully.

Lew Christmas ran the livery stable; a large cavern of blackness now, where horses stamped lazily in serried stalls, and sweet odors of hay and alfalfa, of pungent leather and freshly curried animals came out to meet one. A shaded lamp shed yellow light in the dusty office, and in there wizened Lew Christmas was playing cribbage with a friend.

"Seen a gent named Morley?" Monte asked.

"Morely?" Christmas repeated, cupping his cards jealously, peering over the top of his steel-framed spectacles. "Sure! Hired him a hoss and saddle coupla hours ago. Said he figured to ride out tonight."

"Where?"

"No say. Friend of yours, Monte?"

"Met him. Did he pack a gun?"

"Now you speak of it, I seen so. Somethin' wrong?"

"Not with Morely," said Monte casually. "Slap our saddles on a couple of good horses, Lew." They left.

Manuel Ortega, Crosby's slavish deputy, was dozing in Crosby's leather-backed office chair, legs slanted high on Crosby's desk. Monte smacked him on the shoulder.

"¡Arriba, barracho!" he shouted. "Up, drunkard!"

Ortega left the chair in a wild spring and staggered to the middle of the room, rubbing his eyes. "You mak' thee joke weeth me, eh?" he demanded crossly, scowling. "You theenk that ees fonnee?"

"Sad, but so. We want our guns. Trot 'em out."

"I know nothing about thees guns," Ortega denied, scowling.

Monte eyed Ortega. He liked the deputy little better than Crosby. The two of them were stamped out of the same mold. Crosby was overbearing and scheming, Ortega sly and scheming.

"Jump an' get 'em, you onery sinner!" Monte ordered abruptly. "Or there's gonna be heap grief for one *mejicano* deputy."

Ortega hesitated, still scowling, then sullenly walked to the desk and jerked open the bottom drawer. From it he took two belts with holsters and guns.

"Correct," approved Monte, taking them, handing one to Chris. "An' I reckon we'll take Johnny Simpson's gun, too. Fork it out."

"*Señor* Seempson have come an' get his gun," Ortega said promptly. "I stand here w'en he come in queeck an' ask for heem. An' I give thee gun to heem. An' *Señor* Seempson tek' hees gun an' go out. *¡Verdad!* It is thee truth!"

Monte hooked his thumbs in his cartridge belt. "You wouldn't lie to me, would you, Ortega?"

"For w'y I mak' thee lie to you, *Don* Montee? *Madre de Dios* . . . Mother of God, w'y I do that?"

"Where's Crosby?"

"*¿Quién sabe?* I have been esleep."

"Esleep," said Chris dreamily. "Esleep like a little baby . . . innocent an' harmless as a coyote. He wouldn't lie, Monte. You want I should throw the fear of God into him?"

"*¡Señores!*" warned Ortega, stepping back in alarm. "I am thee law! Eet weel mean gr-reat troble eef you toch me!"

"Come on," said Monte gruffly, turning on his heel.

His mind arranged the facts as they went toward the livery stable. Johnny had his gun. Morely was out of town. Crosby was gone, too. How had Johnny gotten that gun, when Crosby knew about him? Probably Crosby had not told Ortega about Johnny, and, when he had found Johnny had gotten his gun and gone, had tipped off Morely, and the two of them had started after Johnny.

Johnny had said he would not be taken, and he'd meant it! Monte guessed that the matter was moving to a dangerous climax. Embezzlement back in Ohio was one thing for Johnny to face. A shooting scrape on the Huachaca range was another.

He told his fears to Chris.

"How are we going to stop it now?" Chris queried doubtfully. "They got a big start on us."

"Ride," said Monte briefly. "Like as not Crosby an' Morely'll take their time. Figure on trappin' Johnny around daybreak at Wonder Wells. We can take the short cut through Mesa Muerte."

"Death Mesa? Think we can make it at night?"

"Can try."

"Can do, then," said Chris.

Hoofs struck sharply on the stones of Gila Street, rang hollowly on the crossing boards of the railroad track, thudded softly in the dirt beyond. The lights, the buildings, the cottonwoods, and the gaunt black water tank of Huachaca fell behind. Chill night folded in about them.

Crystal stars twinkled gravely down through the cold clear night. The rhythmic cadence of steadily trotting hoofs drummed gently on the stillness. They attempted no long, mad gallops. It would not have made sense. Wonder Wells lay a long and weary way before them.

Three hours out, a sheer black dike barred their way, stretching far into the night on either side. Hoofs rang sharply on the hard rock, clicked briskly over the crests. They changed to Indian file, Monte before, Chris behind. They rode on, twisting, turning, groping forward, past yawning fissures, black and deep. The moon climbed high. The pale, false dawn pushed up into the east. Then dawn, and brightening light that turned to crimson, shot with reaching hands of gold. The sun cocked a warm, inquiring eye above Ladrón Peak and heaved its blazing smile into the sky.

"Hello!" said Monte, reining up. "We ain't the first that passed this way tonight. Another horse."

The sign was plain and fresh. "Crosby, right enough," said Chris. "He started late an' took the short cut."

They topped a rise and looked into the long, low dip beyond.

"What's that?" Chris wondered.

Two horses waited there, and two horsemen stood looking at something on the white sands of the twisting draw.

They were grizzled Ike Evans of the Lazy Hat outfit and young Cisco Lucero of the Lucero clan, half a day's ride beyond the Lazy Hat holdings.

"Buenos días," Cisco greeted. "You ride early this morning, *amigos*."

"Don't we all?" Monte said coolly as he swung down from the saddle and stared at the body on the dry sand at their feet. No need to look a second time, to scan the down-turned face. Jonathan Morely of Ashton, Ohio, would never ride again.

"Who did this?" Monte asked sharply.

Ike Evans spoke sharply: "I hate to say it, but the facts are plain . . . Johnny Simpson."

"You know a heap," Chris blurted. "How come . . . second sight?"

"Crosby told us. Met him down the trail a ways, ridin' hard for Wonder Wells. Told us Johnny was wanted back East. Got out of town tonight with his gun before they could stop him. This feller had come for him, an' rode after him. Crosby followed later. Found this. Johnny shot him and high-tailed for Wonder Wells. Reckon he figured Crosby'd stay behind an' he'd have time to get him a pack an' break for it. The young fool!"

Monte felt dispirited. The night of steady riding was wasted. Johnny, hot-headed, desperate, had bungled everything.

"Damn!" said Chris heavily. "Poor Mary. Crosby'll get him sure now."

"Sí," agreed Cisco Lucero. "Crosby swore by hees hair he

would bring Johnnee Seempson back, alive or dead, for thees killing."

"You two didn't go with him?" Monte asked.

Ike Evans shook his head. "Offered to, but Crosby said we wasn't needed. Vowed he'd do that part all right." Ike nodded at the body. "Poor devil . . . he didn't have a chance. Johnny plugged him three times. Once in the face an' twice in the hollow."

Monte lighted a cigarette, looked sharply at Ike and Cisco. Then he shot a glance at Chris and took another long look at the body. His dusty face was a study. Gradually his eyes hardened. His mouth drew into a thin, tight line. His voice was cold, urgent.

"Ike . . . Cisco, ride with us! Quick! There'll be another killing!"

Ike spat. "I was thinkin' that, too. Crosby took a big job on his hands when he went after Johnny alone. Johnny's a killer now. He'll get Crosby if he can. Cisco, we'd better ride an' take a hand."

The sun was rimming Paloduro Peaks against the turquoise sky. The dusty trail was sucking early morning warmth. A slender yucca, topped with snowy flowers, bobbed greeting to their rush. A lean coyote slid ghost-like into a wash and vanished. Monte saw none of that as he slashed the romal over his horse's heaving side. The horse, feeling the bite of leather rein ends, laid his barrel chest close to the ground, showing for the first time how he could run. Monte threw a glance over his shoulder and saw the others dropping back.

The trail was rocky, steep, and winding. His horse's plunging hoofs tattooed the morning quiet. Far and small against a line of distant cottonwoods two horsemen trotted into view.

"Dear Lord," begged Monte, "give me time!"

The others were just starting down the trail as Monte's horse pointed up the cañon and dug his hoofs into that last fraction of a mile. Some hundred yards had dropped behind when the thin sharp crack of a shot came from ahead.

"Hi, yippety, hoss . . . step it!"

That shrill yell, the whistling romal slashing hard, wrung more speed from Monte's horse's bulging muscles. Half a mile ahead one horse had swerved aside and was galloping at a tangent to the trail, out toward the cañon wall, on toward Monte.

Its rider had slipped from the saddle and was clinging to one side with an arm around the horse's neck, one leg over the saddle. There he was partly shielded from the man who galloped madly after, shooting as he came.

The first horse stumbled, pitched forward, went down in a cloud of dust—down on its clinging rider! No—he kicked clear, fell hard, rolled up into a crouching run, zigzagging as he went. Riding him down, thumbing cartridges into his empty revolver, came Crosby.

Monte shot once, wide, in warning. His shout rang after. "Don't do it, Crosby!"

Johnny Simpson's plunging roan came opposite. Monte swerved his horse in around him, then reined his own horse up in a rearing stop before Crosby. Gun held easy at his knee, Monte smiled thinly.

" 'Mornin', Sheriff. Now who'd have thought we'd meet you out here so soon?"

"Out of my way!" Crosby roared. "What do you mean, shooting at me? I'll jail you for this!"

Monte's gun lifted, steadied. He leaned forward, grinning, but his eyes were cold. "Goodness gracious Agnes, you're all in a lather, Sheriff. It don't become the dignity of the law.

Besides, it's reckless. I rattle easy. Now if you was to shout just once too often, an' I jumped, and my finger slipped on the trigger, that'd come under the head of suicide, wouldn't it?"

"I've no reason for gun play with you, Davis," Crosby said hoarsely. "That man over there is under arrest for murder, and he was escaping. I'll take you for an accessory."

Monte stepped his horse around so he could look back down the cañon and still keep an eye on the sheriff. Johnny Simpson was standing there. The others were riding up.

"I guess the sun's in my eyes," Monte sighed. "First time I ever saw a prisoner escape by standing still. Or mebbe it's in your eyes, Crosby. Drop your bean-shooter an' we'll ride over and ask Johnny what he's doing. If he says escaping, we'll give him a calling down. It ain't good manners."

"I'll see you damned before I do," Crosby gritted.

"Drop it, you double-crossing old vulture! I feel a sneeze coming on, an' something tells me I'll shoot you by accident if you've still got that gun in your hand."

Monte's mouth opened, as if to sneeze.

Crosby paled, dropped his gun. "You'll regret this!" he promised thickly. "I'll make this territory too small to hold you! I'll. . . ."

Monte's threatened sneeze turned into a yawn. He holstered his revolver, smiling. "Save your breath, Crosby. I know your little song. There ain't nothing too dirty for you when you've got your gang behind you. Let's go on over to Johnny there. He's walked far enough."

Chris, Ike Evans, and Cisco Lucero had reined up beside Johnny as Monte and the sheriff came up.

"Evans, I call you and Lucero to witness that this man stopped me in the performance of my duty and disarmed me at the point of his gun!" Crosby cried angrily. "I deputize you both to help arrest him and his partner."

Cisco Lucero laughed softly. "*Gracias* for thee honor w'at you do me, but I don' care to be deputee. *Don* Montee ees wan dangerous man. Me, I tr-remble w'en he r-roll hees cold eye at me." Cisco veiled a wink at Monte.

Crosby's face was purple now. "Evans, you're not yellow, too?"

"Hold your hosses!" Ike Evans snapped. "No man can call me yellow, 'specially when I just seen him turn yellow hisself. Shovel up your own mess!"

"The votes now being counted, the party in office is throwed out on his ear," Monte said cheerfully. "Johnny, what happened?"

"I was bringing him under arrest for murder, and he made a break to get away!" Crosby roared.

"You've been throwed out on your ear," Monte chided. "Silence before something terrible happens to you."

Johnny Simpson's face was a startled study. "First time I heard that story," Johnny told them. "Crosby showed up with a warrant. There wasn't any argument. Mary wanted to ride with us, but Crosby told her she'd better come in later. We had reached the cottonwoods back there when I saw you coming down the trail, Monte. Crosby told me to ride offside quick. There was trouble. I hadn't gone fifty feet when he shot at me. Nicked my shoulder. I slid over in the saddle on the other side of the horse, Indian way. Guess it saved me." Johnny shook his head in perplexity. "But this murder talk . . . I don't savvy that."

"He's lying!" Crosby said viciously. "You men saw the body. Never was a clearer case. His wife'll lie, too, of course. . . ."

"Damn your filthy mouth!" Johnny shouted, clubbing his gun as he sprang at the sheriff.

Monte blocked him with his horse, calmly reached over, and drove Crosby reeling in the saddle with a mighty slap.

"One thing you can't do is trail your foulness on a good woman's name," he said contemptuously. "No, Johnny, leave him be. I'll handle him. Better give me that gun."

"It's not loaded," Johnny said, handing it up.

"I'm not armed," Crosby reminded thickly. "And that gun of his is plenty proof. Look at it."

Monte broke Johnny's revolver, twirled the cylinder. There were five shells, all discharged.

"It's my gun, but he toted it with him," Johnny explained. "Handed it to me as we rode off. I thought it was funny at the time."

"Another lie!" Crosby snarled.

Monte extracted the shells and held them in his palm for a moment, turning each one over, then contemplated Crosby. "Got your handcuffs along?" he questioned mildly.

"Why . . . yes."

"And you didn't handcuff Johnny when you took him back for murder?"

"I . . . I thought he'd be all right."

"Didn't handcuff him, an' let him have his gun? Crosby," said Monte casually, "I reckon you've dug your own trap. Now I'll tell you what really happened, Genesis to Revelations. Ohio came in town with a warrant for Johnny, looked you up, told you his story. You knew Johnny was in town an' didn't make a move. Why?"

"I don't know what you're talking about," Crosby blustered.

"Said the chicken to the fox. Two thousand dollars reward for Johnny . . . two thousand that Ohio man would get. So you scum a scheme. Didn't tell the little stranger his man was right there under his nose. Told him to wait, I expect. Then

Johnny, slipping away, made it perfect. You sent Ohio hoppin' out to Wonder Wells after him. An' you told Ortega to swear Johnny had come an' got his shootin' iron. Then you slipped outta town with Johnny's gun an' yours an' made tracks across Dead Man Mesa last night. Came out on the trail ahead of Ohio, waited there, an' shot him with Johnny's gun. Then you rode on to Wonder Wells, arrested Johnny on the Ohio charge, an' started back with him . . . alone . . . careful not to have Mary along for a witness. Why? Johnny wasn't ever going back to Huachaca, Crosby! You gave him his gun, knowing it was empty. You didn't handcuff him. And when you saw me coming, it forced your hand, your plan to kill Johnny an' claim it was in the line of duty."

"No!" Crosby cried hoarsely.

"Yes," said Monte coldly. "Double murder, an' a sweet slick scheme. Nobody but you could have figured it out. Natural thing for Johnny to shoot a man there on the trail who tried to arrest him. Natural thing for you to follow, find the body, arrest Johnny, then have to shoot him when he made a break for it. A dead Johnny would carry the blame for the dead Ohio. An' you produce dead Johnny and collect that two thousand reward. All the witnesses gone an' not a loophole in your story."

"God," said Johnny thinly. "So that's what he was up to?"

"*Dios* . . . w'at a *muy malo hombre* . . . very bad man, indeed," Cisco Lucero murmured.

"You can't make up a crazy yarn like that an' get sensible men to believe it!" Crosby shouted. "Only a fool would listen to you!"

Ike Evans shook his head. "You're guessin' a heap, Monte," he said dubiously.

"Mebbe so. Chris an' I found Crosby's sign on Mesa Muerte, where he cut through. We directed Ohio to his office from the train. Plenty of time then for Crosby to gather Johnny in. It ain't in reason for Johnny to have called at Crosby's office an' got his gun, because we warned him he was wanted and to slip out of town quick. Ohio gave it away to me in the Atlantic House bar. That gun business had me stumped when Ortega told us. Then when I saw the dead man, I thought, sure, Johnny had done it. Thought so until you said he had been shot three times. That cleared it. Johnny couldn't have. He didn't do any buying in town. Guess the stores will settle that. And when he went in town, he had only one cartridge left. Chris an' me can swear to that. *One*. Even if he'd got his gun an' hightailed it last evening, he *couldn't* have shot his man three times. Crosby bungled his arithmetic. He slipped some of his own shells in Johnny's gun. I've got 'em here. One Winchester Forty-Four . . . that was Johnny's . . . four Remington Forty-Fours . . . those were Crosby's gifts. Look in his belt. You'll see." Monte regarded the sheriff. "Crosby, you white-livered, mealy-mouthed, double-crossing son of a she-rattler, you overplayed your hand! Five aces brand any man a crook, an' they make you a killer! Drag out your handcuffs, because you're going back under arrest, and hang!"

And Crosby went.

Gambler's Lady

Following the Second World War, T. T. Flynn's agent, Marguerite E. Harper, wanted him increasingly to write for the slick magazine market where the pay was much better. Other Harper clients like Fred Glidden who wrote as Luke Short and Jonathan Glidden who wrote as Peter Dawson had successfully made this transition. The story that follows, titled "Rascal on the River" by Flynn, was completed on June 11, 1946. His agent sold it to *The American Magazine*, a monthly published by the Crowell-Collier Corporation which also published *Collier's*. It appeared in the March, 1947 issue under the title "Gambler's Lady." That title has been retained for its first book appearance. T. T. Flynn was paid $3,150.00 for this story, a princely sum compared to what he was being paid by pulp magazines.

The tall young man rode a foam-flecked roan gelding toward Oakport Landing on the lower Mississippi. Mid-morning sunlight struck brightly on cotton fields that stretched away like warm banks of snow. Negroes looked up from picking as the fast-passing rider drew dust along the rough back-country road.

Woodland gave way to fields again. The tall young rider slowed the blowing horse and stopped in front of a white man, leaning against a half-filled cotton wagon beside the road. "How far to the river?" he inquired politely.

"Nice critter under you, suh. Had one to match him when I follered Jeb Stuart."

"Ah . . . you were with Stuart?"

"Yep. Seen ol' Jeb go down at the Yaller Inn, near Richmond. Hit were a sorry day."

"It was that. And the river?" the tall rider reminded, gathering the reins.

"Ain't fur, the way you been ridin'." Shrewd eyes estimated horse and rider. "Live in these parts, mister?"

"I'm passing through. Thank you." A lifted hand, a nod, a heel touch, and the gelding surged into a mile-eating stride.

The farmer looked after the receding dust. "Tryin' to keep ahead, he means. Wonder how fur ahead, an' who's follerin' him." He looked, but the road was empty the way the tall stranger had come.

The sun poised at high noon when the tired roan entered Oakport Landing. The dusty center street passed a cotton gin, weathered brick and frame mercantile buildings, and ended abruptly at a low bluff. A cut in the sandy bluff led down to a small wharf barge. There, at the bluff edge, the stranger reined up and scanned the river. South through shimmering heat the broad channel swept out of sight in a western bend. Northward not even a smoke smudge from some distant steamer touched the clear sky. But south, less than a mile off, a steamboat was blowing for the landing. The deep, delayed blast drifted up the current. Townsmen were already hurrying toward the downward cut in the sandy bluff.

To the right a blacksmith shop faced the bluff edge. The tall stranger rode there and dismounted. The square-faced smith left his anvil. A Negro boy at the handle of the leather bellows turned, gaping.

The stranger started to unsaddle. "Lost a shoe back on the

road. Better give him new ones all around. He'll need water and feed after he's cooled off. I wish your boy would rub him down good. This horse will be called for by someone later in the day."

"I reckon I can do all that, suh. Live around here?"

"No," the tall stranger said, not unpleasantly. "Will ten dollars be agreeable for the accommodation?"

"Good Lord, suh! We ain't robbers in this town."

"Give my horse the best treatment and it's worth it." The stranger's quick smile erased a stern intentness he had brought to the river bluff. "Has there been another upriver boat today?"

"Two boats, suh. The *Kate Sands* come in early, then later on the *Coldriver* stopped. She ain't much, though. That 'un puttin' in now is the *Royal Anne*. She's one of the best."

"I know her," said the stranger briefly. He had the saddle off, and he lifted heavy saddlebags effortlessly. "A man I know may have taken the *Kate Sands* or the *Coldriver*," he said thoughtfully. "Perhaps you saw him. About my size, you might say he favors me."

The smith nodded. "You know, suh, it's been naggin' me. I thought I'd seen you som'eres. It was that feller you speak of. He stood on the bluff there afore breakfast, waitin' for the *Kate Sands* to put in. He went aboard her."

"Nice observation. I thank you."

The smith said: "Don't need to hurry. Old Bill Siler, captain of the *Anne*, has got him a daughter here in Oakport. He 'most always takes time to visit a little with her and her kids. Passengers that don't like the wait c'n unload and walk. Old Siler's stubborn."

"I'm acquainted with Captain Siler's peculiarities," said the stranger, smiling slightly. He started toward the cut in the sandy bluff, heavy leather saddlebags over one arm.

The smith remembered and lifted his voice: "Who shall I give this horse to?"

The stranger stopped, considering. "He'll give you his name," he said, and he went on.

A man like the tall stranger was one to attract attention, no matter where he passed. Here at Oakport Landing it was the more obvious. Eyes were on him as soft, hand-lasted boots carried him down through the dust of the cut. His dark broadcloth suit cried cut and quality. His fine cambric shirt with ruffled front held a diamond stud, and diamond cuff links glinted in the midday sun.

It might have been a bright glint off the cuff diamonds that caught attention from the young lady who sat on an upturned box at one end of the small wharf. She spoke urgently to the dark-skinned maid who stood beside her: "Letty, is it . . . ? No, it isn't! I thought for a second. . . ."

"Sho' do favor him, Miss Jenny. But 'tain't. He lookin' to us now. See . . . don't know us."

The tall stranger was preoccupied as he came on the wharf boat. He glanced at a gold watch impatiently as the steamboat worked in.

At the same moment Colonel Roscoe Bellinger, of Memphis, stood on the hurricane deck of the *Royal Anne* and spoke indignantly to the younger man at his left: "Notice that rascal with the saddlebags, Richard? Don't play cards with him or associate with him."

Richard frowned and smoothed a silky brown mustache. "I've won money from worse-looking rascals. After all, I'm twenty-four, Uncle."

"Twenty-four fools, at times, young man, I'm sorry to say of my nephew."

"What's wrong with him?"

"Wrong with him?" repeated Colonel Bellinger. His face grew redder. "The man's a professional gambler. A desperado, no doubt. Why, last fall, on the boat from New Orleans, he almost drew a gun on me."

"Oh, ho! You were in a card game?"

"To my regret, yes, young man. That rascal professed to be one Clay Rivers, a Saint Louis businessman. I know more about him now. Made it my business to find out."

Bells were ringing below; the ponderous side wheels threshed in the cavernous boxes. Negroes waited with ropes ready as the pilot brought the *Royal Anne* skillfully to her landing. Richard studied the tall stranger with heightened interest.

"So, you mean to expose him, Uncle?"

"I'll use my information in good time," Colonel Bellinger promised stiffly. "I never forget an injury. You'll do well to cultivate a little iron in your backbone, also."

"Jove!" Richard exclaimed. "See that young lady with the maid? Delightful, isn't she? I do believe we'll have her aboard."

"Stop trying to talk like an Englishman! You're a Tennessee planter's son! That's good enough for any man, suh!"

"No doubt," agreed Richard carelessly. "Gad! She *is* coming aboard."

"Keep away from her. You got into enough petticoat trouble in New Orleans!" Colonel Bellinger glared over the rail, and stalked away.

The tall stranger came aboard immediately, ignoring the gaping deck passengers, white and black. He paused, looking back intently at the sandy bluff. Then he went up the broad staircase to the lavish cabin of the *Royal Anne*.

Captain Siler was a small man with a white chin beard, snapping blue eyes, and blunt talk, even to the most distinguished passengers. Now, coming out of the clerk's office, Captain Siler's look frosted a little at sight of the new passenger.

"A pleasure to be on the *Royal Anne* again, Captain." Clay Rivers's smile said he doubted the captain's pleasure. He dropped the saddlebags on the thick carpet. The dull *thud* made their weight obvious.

Captain Siler put a suspicious look on the bags. "This is all the baggage you have, Mister Rivers?"

"I left a horse on shore. You don't, I seem to recall, have cabin accommodations for equine passengers. And, by the way, Captain, I'm reminded you usually dally for some reason here at Oakport Landing."

"If you mean visiting my daughter and grandchildren, yes, Mister Rivers. Good day, sir, and I'll not look kindly on any unpleasant occurrences this trip."

"Naturally. Could you use a little extra money this trip?"

Captain Siler turned back, challenge in his manner. "I've had money offered before, Mister Rivers! Some offers I don't take kindly, sir!"

Clay's smile was mostly with his lips. They had this end of the long, spacious saloon to themselves. "I'll take it pleasantly, Captain, that you don't impugn my integrity, at cards or otherwise."

"I ain't impugning anything, Mister Rivers."

"Thank you. I have a little sporting offer. The *Kate Sands* put in here about breakfast time. Could you overtake the *Kate* somewhere between here and Memphis for, say, a sporting thousand, in gold?"

Captain Siler was shaking his head brusquely until he heard the two final words. He stared. "This some kind of trick, Mister Rivers?"

"An unfortunate choice of words, Captain. Gold speaks

quite clearly." The dusty toe of an expensive boot stirred one of the heavy saddlebags.

"You must have weighty reason for coming up with the *Kate Sands*, Mister Rivers."

"Nothing that good gold won't explain, Captain. Or perhaps there's a boat following you that's more suitable for a sporting run."

"Captain Lewis and the *Cherokee* should be six or seven hours behind us," Captain Siler admitted. He dismissed the *Cherokee*'s speed with a shrug. "A thousand!" he muttered. "Very well. We leave in about ten minutes. Mister Cranshaw, the clerk, will arrange your passage."

Captain Siler hurried down to the freight dock. His brusque shouts to the mate drifted back. Smiling faintly, Clay Rivers had a word with Cranshaw, the clerk, and then went up to the high texas deck, where he could watch the wharf boat and the Oakport bluff.

There, for the first time, weariness settled on him. He lighted a long, thin cigar with sensitive fingers and leaned indolently against the white rail.

Negro roustabouts were singing as they carried freight ashore. Captain Siler stood on the wharf boat, talking to a buxom woman who held a baby. Four more children of assorted sizes milled around their mother and grandfather. Townspeople watched from the wharf boat and the bluff edge.

Clay Rivers was a somber and detached figure at the texas rail, so much so that several male passengers who might have joined him abandoned the impulse. It was the young woman with the dark-skinned maid who intruded on his aloofness. She did it unintentionally by pausing at the rail near him.

Clay became aware of the girl's presence without interest. The tall maid was standing behind her mistress. Clay vaguely recalled seeing them on the wharf boat. He noted the finely formed silhouette of the girl's face, the full curve of her lips in the shadow cast by her perky straw bonnet.

She did not seem to mind the full strike of midday sunshine. Clay guessed absently she was no stranger to sidesaddle and sun-drenched rides. Her hand rested on the rail, and he marked a gold wedding band.

The maid cut a glance at him, saw he noticed, and looked stonily at her mistress's bonnet. Her mistress glanced, also, a moment later and met Clay's look, and after an indecisive moment spoke impersonally.

"Did I understand the captain to give orders to leave as soon as possible?"

"Quite correct, ma'am." Clay glanced up at the two tall stacks. They were pouring dark smoke. "Captain Siler's decided on a fast run upriver."

Clay thought she looked relieved. Her lashes were long. The promise of her silhouette was redeemed by the rest of her face. He guessed she might be worth talking to, with a minimum of nonsense chatter.

The maid jumped, squealed, as the big, deep-toned bell rang warning of the boat's departure. Her mistress put out a quick, reassuring hand. When quiet fell, Clay heard the maid: "Jes' couldn't he'p it, Miss Jenny. 'Scuse me, ma'am."

There was, Clay guessed, worship and fierce affection in that maid for her mistress. Like reading a stranger across a card table, Clay built his knowledge. The mistress's name was Jenny. She was kind, thoughtful, likable. That pleased him. He had thought something of the sort at first sight.

Smiling, the girl said to Clay: "This is Letty's first trip on a steamboat. She expects to be on the bottom or blown up by the boilers before we're in mid-river."

"I assure your maid, ma'am, nothing of the sort will

happen," Clay said. "Captain Siler is half owner. He can't afford to let such a thing happen."

"You see, Letty?" she said, and then added quickly: "Now, that's only the engines starting."

Letty relaxed doubtfully. The great paddle wheel below them was churning in the paddle box. The *Royal Anne* worked clear and swung toward the channel.

Clay watched the bluff recede. Tension began to leave him. The widening gap between boat and shore seemed to end some urgent need for watchfulness. Then, abruptly, his manner hardened expectantly. Six men on horseback had ridden to the bluff edge. Three of the men swung out of their saddles. Across the hot, bright shimmer of noon they could be seen speaking excitedly to the townspeople who still lingered at the bluff.

One man cupped his hands to his mouth and shouted after the steamer. The threshing paddle wheels, the steady *chuff-chuff* of the escape pipe, the engine noise on the lower deck, reduced the full-shouted hail on shore to a blurred thread of sound.

Clay's intent watchfulness was broken by a light touch on his arm. The girl had stepped beside him. She, too, was watching the bluff. She asked, a bit breathlessly: "Aren't they calling the boat back?"

"It seems so, ma'am."

"Will the captain turn back?"

Bells rang below. "Captain Siler seems to have some notion of taking them aboard. I'll ask him, ma'am. You'll pardon me?"

He left the saddlebags there by the rail, going forward with strides that were leisurely deceptive, so swiftly did they carry him toward the ornate pilot house atop the texas.

Captain Siler was stepping out of the pilot house with a

small, battered speaking trumpet when Clay faced him: "Trouble, Captain?"

"Passengers missed the boat," Siler said testily. "Reckon they figured on me stopping for a while, like I usually do." He lifted the trumpet to hail the bluff.

Clay said coldly: "My thousand dollars won't appreciate a delay, Captain."

"Won't take long," Siler said impatiently.

"I insist!"

A flush surged into Captain Siler's face. Ready temper stiffened his spare figure. "I'm captain of this boat, Mister Rivers!"

"Quite so." Clay's smile was bleak. "I'm captain of those saddlebags and contents. Today I'm not feeling generous toward late passengers from Oakport Landing."

Siler lowered the trumpet. "So that's the way? You don't care to have those men aboard?"

"If you'll have it so."

"Perhaps," said Siler, still flushed, "you're more interested in getting away from Oakport Landing than you are in coming up with the *Kate Sands*?"

"I've not said so." Clay's impersonal stare met Siler's angry look. "There's a thousand in the game, Captain. Are you calling me?"

Hard-headed business took command of Siler's emotion. "We'll go on, Mister Rivers. I'm not interested in your reasons."

"Thank you, Captain."

Siler swung back into the pilot house. The bleak look clung on Clay's face as he retraced his steps.

Other passengers on the texas dock gave curious glances as he returned. Clay ignored them. Engine-room bells started the wheels churning again. The *Royal Anne* thrust ahead into the current as Clay rejoined the girl and her maid.

"The captain," Clay said calmly, "decided not to turn back." She seemed to be relieved, and he asked: "Do you know those men who wanted to come aboard?"

She looked past him at the figures growing smaller on the bluff edge. Her hesitation could have been uncertainty. "I thought one of them was familiar."

"The gentleman's name, ma'am?"

Again her slight pause. "He would be Squire Beckford, of Ophir Creek Plantation."

"Beckford?" Clay said reflectively. "I don't believe I have the pleasure. Seems to me I've heard of Ophir Creek Plantation. Is it your home, ma'am?"

"Ophir Creek is well known to me, sir." She noted Clay's glance at the wedding band. Her look went to the maid, faintly smiling at some thought that flashed between them. "My home now," she said, "is Virginia. Fairhill Plantation, on the James River."

"A beautiful section, ma'am," Clay assured her. "I've passed through and admired that James River country." He paused, thinking, while his eyes estimated the Oakport bluff. "I'm trying to recall Fairhill Plantation," he said. "Seems to me I've heard the name and the owner's name."

"No doubt," she assented. "The owner was quite well known with Lee. Captain George Siddon Cockburn."

"Yes," Clay said, nodding. "An old and distinguished family in those parts, I remember being told. And you, ma'am, are Missus Cockburn?" Her hand moved on the rail, bringing his attention to the yellow gold band. Clay bowed slightly. "With your permission, ma'am, I'm Mister Clay Rivers, of Saint Louis. Since you seem to be traveling alone, may I place myself at your service?"

She said: "Thank you. I'm joining Captain Cockburn in

Memphis. He'll be pleased to thank you, also."

She had the impersonal pleasantness of travelers in casual contact. Equally casually she nodded and left him there at the rail. The tall, thin, dark-skinned maid followed her silently.

Clay sensed again the fierce, dogged protection of maid for mistress. He looked back toward the shore pensively. A long time he stood there in the hot sunlight, watching the panorama of riverbank sliding back downriver.

Oakport Landing was long out of sight when Clay finally admitted weariness of bone and muscle, and a weariness of spirit, too, that unaccountably had seized him. He carried the heavy saddlebags below, and very quickly was stretched on clean, smooth sheets in his own small cabin. Sleep was almost instant.

Dusk hovered outside when Clay stepped again into the long, luxurious saloon. White-coated waiters had set up the dining tables and were busy with linen and silver. Crystal chandeliers blazed with light. He smiled faintly as he looked at the familiar luxury. There was no mode of travel in the country so splendid and comfortable as these fine Mississippi packets.

By the feel of the engines pulsing through the long hull, Clay judged the *Royal Anne* was driving at top speed. A thought struck him. He questioned a waiter, and he walked the length of the saloon and found a steward known to him.

Passing a gold coin idly from palm to palm, Clay suggested: "It struck me there might be a vacant seat at Missus Cockburn's table."

The steward looked at the gold piece. His slight nod brought the money into his hand. He smiled. "You're the second gentleman who's made the request, Mister Rivers."

"And the other gentleman, Henry?"

"A Mister Richard Bellinger, from Memphis, sir. The young gentleman came aboard at New Orleans." Henry coughed to mask amusement. "There seemed no harm in changing his seat, sir."

"The conversation should be livelier," Clay agreed, smiling.

The first few minutes of dinner left something to be desired in the conversation. By accident or design, the steward had discreetly balanced Mrs. Cockburn's table of four with a full-bosomed, iron-visaged matron who sat beside young Mrs. Cockburn. Clay was the last one seated. He noted with amusement that young Richard Bellinger was restless as the matron held him in conversation. Young Bellinger did not look happier when Clay was placed beside him.

Young Mrs. Cockburn seemed slightly startled at finding Clay at her table. Her nod was pleasant enough. Clay introduced himself. The matron's name, he was informed firmly, was Mrs. Henry van Dyke. She was in the midst of a determined cross-examination of young Bellinger, when she switched to Clay.

"Saint Louis was my home for a number of years," she stated, and dropped an aside to Mrs. Cockburn: "I was a bride in Saint Louis, my dear. You wouldn't know the city as it was then." And then she asked Clay: "Do you know the Judge Slocum family, young man?"

"I don't believe so, ma'am."

"The Garrisons who have the lumber mill?"

"I believe I have heard of young Philip Garrison."

"Very prominent family," commented Mrs. van Dyke with some satisfaction. "What business did you say you were in?"

"I didn't say, ma'am." Clay calmly folded his napkin. He

thought that Bellinger was maliciously pleased at the trend of the talk. There was no denying young Mrs. Cockburn's interest. "Certain aspects of the investment and banking business engage me, ma'am," Clay told Mrs. van Dyke.

"How strange you don't know Judge Slocum. Their bank is, I understand, now one of the largest in Saint Louis."

"Ah, quite so. I thought of the judiciary, ma'am, when you mentioned the judge's name. Our banking is done elsewhere. You don't live in Saint Louis now?"

"I am a resident of Memphis, sir. I was telling Mister Bellinger that I knew his grandfather quite well."

Bellinger touched his soft brown mustache restlessly. "Jove, a pity Grandfather can't be with us tonight!" To young Mrs. Cockburn, Richard said hopefully: "So you're going to Memphis, ma'am? Perhaps we have mutual acquaintances."

"I am not familiar with Memphis, sir," she answered, smiling.

"One never can tell," Richard persisted.

"Your grandfather," said Mrs. van Dyke, "was a most interesting gentleman, young man. Why, I remember. . . ."

The dinner went off like that, the quite formidable Mrs. van Dyke dominating all the talk. Clay ate well, saying little, enjoying discreetly the play of expression on young Mrs. Cockburn's face.

He had a vague regret about the gold band on her finger. Life had seemed full and pleasant. Watching her, Clay had the feeling that life had not been so full, after all. It was pleasant to sit here, thinking of her as the gracious mistress of that James River plantation, in Virginia.

He became aware of young Mrs. Cockburn's disturbing look and realized he'd been staring at her, frowning with concentration. He smiled instantly.

It was not enough. He had disturbed her. A withdrawal

deep in her eyes persisted, like faint alarm and suspicion. Clay regretted it. At the same time he felt a strong wish to overcome her suspicion.

She had eaten lightly and barely touched her dessert. Young Bellinger found a sudden disinclination for dessert, also. He forsook the table when Mrs. Cockburn arose.

"Jove! You must know Memphis, by all means!" was the last Clay heard as Bellinger moved off with her.

Mrs. van Dyke, entrenched behind pastry and thick whipped cream, cast a knowing glance after the two. "Like father, like son," she commented to Clay. "The men of that family can't resist a pretty face, if talk can be believed."

"In this case, ma'am, I'd say the gentleman displays good taste."

"I," said Mrs. van Dyke firmly, "have no wish to disagree with you, Mister Rivers. Still, the world being what it is, one can't approve of young ladies traveling alone."

"I believe she has her maid, ma'am."

"A black girl, Mister Rivers, can't take the place of male members of a young woman's family. If I were her husband. . . ."

Clay put his napkin on the table. His smiling politeness waned in the level look he sent across the table. "If I were Captain Cockburn, madam, I should consider it quite proper for my wife to be on the *Royal Anne* with her maid." Some devil of stubbornness made Clay add: "Indeed, more than proper to be pleasant to a young gentleman who happened to be seated at table with her."

"A gentlewoman who has reached my age sees such things in a different light," Mrs. van Dyke said coldly.

The same devil of perversity drove Clay on as he stood up. "Should I reach that age, ma'am, who knows what my opinion will be."

He bowed, and turned from the formidable-tongued lady who would not be friendly to him from now on. At the moment it did not greatly matter.

Captain Siler had appeared at his table briefly and then disappeared. Clay guessed the captain was about his business of driving the *Royal Anne* as fast as boilers and engines could deliver. A thousand dollars gold was welcome even to the part owner of a steamboat, and there was the sporting side of the *Royal Anne*'s making a record run to overtake the *Kate Sands*.

Night had thrown dark mystery over the broad river. Windows, skylights, engine-room openings were covered to shut in light that might disturb the pilot's cat-like vision. Red sparks whirled out of the tall stacks and vanished astern. Siler was driving her.

Clay paused on the hurricane deck, the wind against his face. A livid shaft of lightning lanced the dark sky ahead. The feel of a thunderstorm was in the breeze. His eyes adjusted to the night, and the long superstructure of the steamboat took form.

Clay made out young Mrs. Cockburn with Richard Bellinger. He had no scruples about joining them.

"When you've heard all about Memphis, ma'am," he offered with some amusement, "I've no doubt descriptions of Saint Louis will also prove interesting."

"Since I'll see Memphis myself," she answered, "perhaps I should hear all about Saint Louis. But tomorrow, if you don't mind. I have a headache and am going to my room."

"A pity, ma'am. Captain Siler has promised to put me aboard another boat by daybreak. The *Kate Sands*."

Far ahead, lightning streaked the sky. The flash showed her quick, questioning look and the sulky features of young Bellinger, who was not relishing the intrusion.

"I was told at Oakport Landing the *Kate Sands* put in early this morning," Mrs. Cockburn said. "Is that why Captain Siler is running so fast? I've heard several people speaking of our speed. To let you go aboard the *Kate Sands,* Mister Rivers?"

"I believe so, ma'am."

"Seems odd to me," Bellinger observed sulkily. "If you're going to Saint Louis, why hurry to catch a slower boat, and one not so comfortable as this?"

"Business," Clay said.

"I suppose someone with a deal of money is aboard the *Kate Sands,*" Bellinger suggested unpleasantly.

Clay thought that over and said softly: "I don't believe I understand you, sir."

"I think you do. Rather fancy yourself at cards, don't you?"

"I play a fair game."

Young Bellinger laughed shortly. "I understand you do quite a bit of gambling on the river. Personally I haven't met the man who could take my money at honest cards."

"Good night, gentlemen," Mrs. Cockburn said.

"I'll see you to the saloon, ma'am," Bellinger offered hastily.

Clay stood frowning. Had he been right about her alarm when the *Kate Sands* was mentioned? Young Bellinger was a nuisance, who had muddled this last chance to talk with her. A sense of loss persisted. Clay went below to the bar and ordered whisky and soda.

He knew the white-coated bartender. The handsomely furnished smoking room of the *Royal Anne* was familiar from other trips. Cigar smoke floated under the lamps in gentle layers. Conversation was lively. Two poker games were in progress.

A bearded gentleman at Clay's elbow suggested: "Would a

few hands of chance interest you, sir?"

"Not at this time, thank you," Clay declined politely, and signaled to the bartender for another drink. Usually he would have joined a poker game with smiling pleasure. Tonight the savor was gone. He had no desire for gambling. Clay knew why.

His thoughts were on that distant Virginia plantation to which young Mrs. Cockburn was traveling. There was a gracious, worthwhile life. Over the second drink Clay wondered moodily what values were in the life through which Clay Rivers had been drifting. He was honest about it. Young Mrs. Cockburn made that far Virginia plantation desirable. Clay scowled at his glass and knew he was scowling at the thought of the lucky husband to whom she was hurrying.

A familiar sulky voice broke into his thoughts: "Mister Rivers might make up the game. He's supposed to be quite a card player. I'm keen to see if he is."

The bearded gentleman, a second stoutish man in a flowered waistcoat, and young Bellinger, had come together. They approached Clay.

"A long evening, suh," the stoutish man boomed. "We only need your pleasure, suh, to have a small and friendly game until bedtime."

Clay put his glass on the bar in abrupt decision. "A pleasure, gentlemen."

The bearded man was a Cairo merchant named McAdams. The big, florid stranger was a cotton shipper from Memphis. The game, Clay quickly saw, was to be more than casual poker for small stakes.

Young Bellinger was making it so. He was a surprisingly good player, bold, reckless. The rather weak and handsome face showed much expression, but, strangely, Richard's face seldom gave away his play. He looked one thing and did another. He handled cards with skill and watched Clay closely, suspiciously. When they bet against each other, Richard usually raised heavily. Clay lost two sizable pots to the young man.

"If this keeps up, you'll have me barefooted," Clay chuckled. The old thrill of a good poker game was back.

An hour later Clay was winning sizably. Richard was forcing bets. The other two men played cautiously, staying about even. Richard called for a drink and gulped it.

"Won't help your game," Clay suggested good-naturedly.

"My game will take care of itself," Richard answered irritably. He dealt, and on his own deal lost some two hundred dollars to Clay's hand.

"You seem to be bringing me luck," Clay said, smiling.

"It's not my intention," Richard retorted irritably. "Sell me some chips."

Clay pushed out the chips. He was reaching for the money when an angry voice broke out behind him: "Richard, I warned you against playing cards with this man!"

Clay looked up. Men at the bar and at other tables ceased talking. The portly red-faced speaker was a stranger.

Clay's memory was slow in recalling an unpleasantness a year ago with this Colonel Bellinger of Memphis. His face smoothed to calm politeness. "You were referring to me, sir?"

"I addressed my nephew! He was warned about sitting in a poker game with you, or associating with you!"

"I see." Clay pushed back the chair and stood up. "You can't hope I'll not resent your remarks."

"Be damned, sir, to what you do! When a man's wife entices my nephew into a poker game. . . ."

"Good heavens, Uncle!" Richard protested. "Rivers is

traveling alone! Stop treating me like a child. I can take care of myself."

"Then do so. You've been puling around that Missus Cockburn all afternoon and evening! Did she suggest you play cards with this man?"

Clay's face tightened. Colonel Bellinger saw it, and loudly warned: "I'll have the captain iron you for a common scoundrel, sir, if you threaten to draw a pistol as you did last year! I know what I'm saying!"

"Omit any lady's name from your conversation here," Clay said so quietly that his repressed threat became a solid and dangerous thing.

Richard's angry bewilderment was laced with uncertain interest. "Seems to me there was some mention from her of occupying the rest of the evening with cards," Richard muttered.

McAdams, the Cairo merchant, was on his feet, also. "I request an explanation, gentlemen!" he said sternly.

Colonel Bellinger answered him loudly: "This man is a Captain Cockburn, of Virginia, although he uses the name of Clay Rivers. The clerk will inform anyone that a lady calling herself Missus Cockburn came aboard with him at Oakport Landing. They dined at the same table with my nephew. It's quite obvious that husband and wife are working together, roping in fools like my nephew."

Clay's mind balanced facts coolly, despite his anger. The damage was done. Shooting the fellow would only make it worse.

Someone must have summoned the captain. Siler was suddenly with them, bristling authority: "Gentlemen, I'll not have trouble on my boat! Mister Rivers, I warn you, knowing your temper."

"Siler," Clay said coldly, "I'm being presented with the

name of Cockburn, and with a wife I never saw until I came aboard your boat today. You've known me. I suggest you clear the lady's name, since I'm denied the pleasure."

Siler was amazed and blunt: "Mister Rivers, you've never mentioned a wife. You've had scant to do with any ladies that I know of."

"I've the lady's reputation in mind." Only in Clay's eyes was his full fury evident. "I say this man lies, maliciously and cowardly, about a lady traveling without protection. You'll see that the good name of a woman on your boat is protected, Captain, or I'll do it for you! D'you hear me?"

Men standing close read Clay's face and began to edge back.

"Hold now, Mister Rivers," Siler said hurriedly. He had been too long on the river not to recognize a crisis. "You and the lady came aboard at Oakport Landing, but that's not proof of anything. Colonel Bellinger, sir, you've made statements that gentlemen aboard can't forgive, without more proof."

Bellinger was choleric and stubborn. He stammered angrily, clawing inside his coat. "Proof? Naturally, I have proof! I've been gathering proof since this man almost drew a gun on me last year in a card game."

"I should have shot you then for your lying charge of cheating," Clay said in white-lipped anger.

"I never forget an injury," Colonel Bellinger said loudly, opening a letter. His hands trembled with emotion. "When an acquaintance mentioned he'd seen an old war comrade who had changed his name from Cockburn to Clay Rivers, I investigated, gentlemen. My lawyers wrote to lawyers in Virginia, where this man Cockburn was from. I read you the reply . . . 'Sir . . . The Captain George Siddon Cockburn, of whom you address inquiry, is well known in this section. He had an enviable record in the late war. Captain Cockburn's Fairhill Plantation, unfortunately, was all but destroyed in the campaign. The captain was seen riding over the property after the peace. He confided in no one and vanished. There was some talk of a letter from California stating that Captain Cockburn had been seen in business there with a man named Ryan. That could be rumor, unsupported by further evidence. I regret, however, to inform you, sir, that in the last two years sundry inquiries have come to this town from peace officers at widely scattered points. A man who at least calls himself Captain Cockburn, of Fairhill Plantation, has been involved in certain unsavory escapades, such as dishonest gambling and outright theft. The writer of this letter finds such reports difficult to believe, considering the high regard in which three generations of the Cockburn family have been held in southern Virginia. Nevertheless, sir, in professional honesty, I send you these reports, which are a matter of public knowledge in this community." Bellinger struck the letter. "Dishonest gambling! Theft!"

"An interesting history of a man named Cockburn," Clay said evenly. "I am Clay Rivers, of Saint Louis. Captain Siler will bear witness. I say that any suggestion I play dishonest cards or have ever stolen so much as a cent is an irresponsible lie. You hear, Bellinger? A lie and a slander!"

"You, sir, are not intimidating me! I've nailed you where you belong! My lawyers also have investigated your Saint Louis connections. You, sir, are the silent partner of one Andrew Ryan, owner of the Donna Belle, in Saint Louis, the most lavish gambling hell between the Appalachians and California! This letter from Virginia, you'll recall, links Captain Cockburn with a Ryan in California. I repeat, my nephew will not be tricked into gambling with you, either by your wife or yourself. I demand that Captain Siler support me."

Clay laughed. Even Colonel Bellinger paused at the sound.

"I've heard no proof of the lady's being dishonest or connected with Clay Rivers of Saint Louis. You were about to apologize for bringing her name into this. Or am I mistaken?"

Colonel Bellinger had had this little drama long planned. Now his bluster quieted at the blazing look on Clay's face.

"As a gentleman, I have no wish to accuse a lady," Colonel Bellinger said thickly. "I stand on this letter from Virginia and public record in Saint Louis. I shall apologize to the lady who, unfortunately, was mentioned somewhat hastily."

"Immediately," said Clay. "In five minutes, exactly, I'll hold you accountable. And I'll have no interference by any man aboard. Furthermore, there was no dishonesty in the card game. Settlement will be made as the chips now stand."

"Do so, Richard, and go to your stateroom!" Colonel Bellinger ordered. He was pale as he walked out.

"The matter is settled, gentlemen," Captain Siler said testily. "Will everyone step to the bar pleasantly at the captain's expense?"

Most of the spectators complied. Others edged out as quickly as they decently could. Clay pocketed his winnings from a sullen and severe McAdams. He guessed the departing men were hurrying to their womenfolk with a story that would set every feminine tongue aboard wagging.

Clay stood by the card table alone, ignoring glances sent his way. When the five minutes were up, he closed the gold repeater watch and strolled slowly into the brilliantly lighted saloon.

A lesser man might have paused. The saloon was the social center of a river packet. Richly decorated and furnished, it extended the length of the boiler deck, staterooms opening on either side. Every woman aboard seemed to have found reason to appear in the long saloon at this moment. The gentlemen, also.

Low-voiced conversation was mostly pretense. All eyes were on the slender figure of young Mrs. Cockburn, at the door of her stateroom, where Colonel Bellinger stood stiffly formal. Clay saw that Jenny Cockburn was reading Bellinger's letter.

Conversation ceased when Clay appeared. Thunder, nearer now, growled through the quiet. Clay was composed as he advanced. He watched Jenny Cockburn, standing straight, pale, intent on the letter she was reading.

She finished and returned the letter, and she saw Clay coming. Her clear voice carried, trembling slightly: "Your apology, sir, is accepted as meant. The man you call Captain Cockburn is not my husband. I think your letter gives the answer you need."

"No doubt, ma'am," Colonel Bellinger replied stiffly, and bowed. "If my apology is accepted, I'll bid you good evening. . . ."

"Wait!"

Clay stopped near them, impassively watching.

Colonel Bellinger looked uncomfortable and wishful of ending the exchange. The dark-skinned maid brooded worriedly inside the stateroom, helpless to aid her mistress. Jenny Cockburn, Clay could have sworn, grew taller inch by inch as she stood there.

"You've seen fit to meddle with the private life of Captain Cockburn," she told the colonel. "I'm quite aware, sir, that Fairhill Plantation was burned while Captain Cockburn was fighting for a cause he thought just. He has told me how, after the peace, sick at heart, he went to California. He is returning, to build again at Fairhill." Her voice had steadied. A disdainful look was about her like a shield, and it put a proud blade in her tone: "Captain Cockburn would not be guilty of dishonesty. It is obvious someone has been impersonating him." She turned the disdainful look on Clay. "Some gambler and rascal," she said, "who must look remarkably like Captain Cockburn. This man is not my husband. Isn't that your answer?"

"The thought hadn't occurred to me," Bellinger blurted.

Her smile had scornful understanding. "I was unfortunate enough to come aboard at Oakport Landing with my maid. Captain Cockburn will meet me at Memphis."

"Of course, ma'am," Bellinger spluttered hastily. "I recall now seeing you and your maid waiting alone. Doubtless you have the answer. I trust the matter will be ended to your satisfaction, and your husband's also, ma'am." Bellinger bowed again, and walked away.

Clay bowed, also, the ghost of a smile at his mouth. "I'm denied a wife," he murmured. "It seems I remain a rascal. Believe me, ma'am, I regret all this."

"You should," Jenny Cockburn said coldly.

Her door closed against his gaze. Clay stood a moment, and then retraced his steps to the bar. No one made an effort to join him.

Clay welcomed the isolation. The stern intentness he had brought to Oakport Landing had returned. His expression did not change when a white-coated Negro appeared at his elbow.

"Cap'n, suh, asks yo' pleasure at de cap'n's cabin on de texas."

Clay nodded and took his time about finishing the drink. He was thoughtful as he went up to Captain Siler's fine quarters and knocked. Siler had taken off his coat, put on carpet slippers, and was smoking a cigar when he opened the door.

"Come in," Siler invited, with less courtesy than he had

always used. Siler, when all was said, was a hard-headed river man. "There's the devil to pay," he commented bluntly when Clay stepped in and the door was closed. "Missus Cockburn has been at me. She's greatly upset."

"No doubt," Clay agreed. His smile was faint. "Being presented with an extra husband would not lull any lady to sleep."

"Can't blame her," Siler growled. "The fingers are waggin' in the saloon. Not a woman aboard but believes Missus Cockburn has some connection with you."

"None of my doing, Captain." Clay was lighting a cigar. "You let that ass, Bellinger, read his letter in public. I did what I could by sending him to her with an apology."

"Pitch pine on the fire," Siler said dryly. "Now, then, Missus Cockburn insists you must be the man who has been impersonating Captain Cockburn. She wants you locked up and turned over to the authorities at Memphis."

"I haven't claimed to be Captain Cockburn."

"Or at least," Siler said, watching sharply, "the lady insists you not be allowed to go aboard the *Kate Sands*. She's afraid her husband is aboard the *Sands*. She thinks you mean to kill him."

"Our bargain was to put me aboard the *Sands*," Clay reminded.

"You brought gold aboard in those saddlebags, Mister Rivers. Men evidently pursued you to the river."

"I don't care to explain anything, Captain. We made a bargain. Is it still in force?"

Siler was shrewd about it: "I'll earn my thousand by coming up with the *Kate Sands* as fast as the boilers will push us. Then, Mister Rivers, I'll talk with the captain of the *Sands*. If he has a Captain Cockburn aboard, I'll warn him of possible trouble."

"You're meddling in matters that are none of your concern, Siler."

"I'll decide my actions aboard my own boat, Mister Rivers."

"Very well," said Clay. "But I warn you."

Thunder upriver rolled loudly. When Clay stepped out into the blackness, the wind was rising and gusty. Lightning showed the river briefly from bank to bank, and a timbered island ahead.

Clay walked forward, something wild and stormy in him rising to meet the coming squall. He had long schooled himself against emotion. Now, in the darkness, with the wind gusts whipping his face, he stood thinking of the past and the future. It seemed natural now, inevitable, that Jenny Cockburn was squarely in those thoughts.

The storm struck. Wind and rain beat at him. There was a stormy satisfaction in facing it. The urgent pulse of the engines vibrated underfoot. Clay smiled faintly at thought of Siler, racing stubbornly through the storm to earn the thousand in gold.

Lightning showed the foot of the island close on the left. The pilot meant to run another cut-off at full speed, saving miles of looping channel. Clay doubted the wisdom of it.

The full storm was on them now. Blinding lightning stuck trees on the starboard bank. The thunder crash shook the night and the *Royal Anne*. The deck heaved and canted, as if shaking mightily from that terrific blast of thunder.

The *Royal Anne* shuddered and swerved off course, heeling far over until the clapper of the great bell struck one booming, mournful note.

Bells jangled in the engine room. The engines stopped. A voice shouted from the wheelhouse. Warning yells burst from roustabouts and deck passengers below. Clay had staggered to the rail. He stood there, guessing the bottom had been ripped by some great snag bedded near the foot of the island.

Such things happened all along the river. Boats by the score had been sunk in just this fashion. The storm howled past. Clay felt the engines reverse.

The *Royal Anne* shuddered under the reverse pull of the big wheels. Slowly she swung broadside to the storm, trying to wrench off the obstruction. The deck slope grew worse as wind beat broadside against the clumsy superstructure.

The pilot, Clay guessed, could not beach on the foot of the island. He might not be able to swing his sluggish, sinking craft to the high shore. Clay turned his back to the storm, stumbling toward the saloon and Jenny Cockburn.

He met panic. Men and women were bolting toward the narrow strip of outside deck. The saloon lights still burned. The luxurious interior, sheltered from the storm, made panic an ugly thing. Many were half dressed. Fright, helplessness, sheer, unreasoning panic were shameful under the bright lights.

The floor canted more noticeably as Clay found Jenny Cockburn's stateroom door open. She was gone. Clay swore softly.

A white-coated Negro fled the length of the saloon, eyes rolling. "She's a-sinkin', white folks! Find de boats! Get in de boats!"

A fat man struggled past with two large carpetbags. Clay remembered the heavy saddlebags in his stateroom. He put them from mind and hurried to the narrow larboard deck, calling: "Missus Cockburn! Jenny Cockburn!"

The wind and beating rain, the cries and confusion blotted his voice. Precious time would be wasted by wandering in the terrified throng. Clay had a vivid thought. It was as if his mind, for an instant, had linked with Jenny Cockburn's mind, understanding clearly what she had done. He pushed with difficulty toward the after end of the *Royal Anne*, where the maid would have retired for the night.

The *Anne* was heeling far over, settling fast. Attempts were being made to lower boats. The storm-ridden sheets of rain lashed crew and passengers into a helpless mass.

At the dark stern Clay found a door open. He groped into a narrow passage, calling.

She was there in the blackness demanding: "Do you know where Letty is?"

Clay caught her arm. It was wet from the storm. "Get outside! You may be trapped in here any minute!"

Jenny Cockburn let Clay draw her out to the rail. Her fright was not for herself, he noted.

"Poor Letty was afraid of this. She won't know what to do!"

"Can she swim?"

"She used to swim in Ophir Creek. Let me go. I must find her!"

Clay held her arms. He had to grip the rail to keep balance on the steeply canting deck. "It's not safe up forward. They'll trample you."

Jenny was trying to go when the boilers blew up. Later, Clay knew that was what had happened. He recalled that the safety valves had not been blowing steam as they should after the engines stopped turning. But when it happened, he was holding to the rail. Jenny was pulling away—and suddenly the explosion erupted and shattered.

One moment Clay held Jenny Cockburn's cold, wet arm; the next he was in space. He struck the water hard and went under. Instinctively he held his breath and started to fight the river.

Clay did not consciously think of Jenny Cockburn. But while he fought the drag of wet clothes and heavy shoes, he had the same fright for her that Jenny must have had for her maid.

He reached the surface and floundered in rain-lashed waves. The fast current caught at him as he cried Jenny's name.

He thought her thin and gasping voice replied, and swam hard toward the sound. His hand struck her shoulder, and he was beside her again, aware of her frantic efforts to keep afloat in sodden clothes. Wind-beaten waves washed over them. Current dragged them fast downstream. Riding the storm above them were screams and helpless cries.

"Keep swimming while I get my shoes off!" Clay gasped.

Slapping water choked Jenny's reply. Clay ducked under, tearing at his shoes. When he kicked them off, he let coat and trousers follow toward the deep bottom.

Wreckage was no longer showering about them. Swimming was easier now. Clay aided Jenny Cockburn. "Get out of that jacket and dress! Get your shoes off! I'll help you!"

Jenny was gasping, choking. She must have been terrified. But she did not catch at him. Clay felt her struggling to take off the jacket. He helped. First the jacket, then the dress. . . . There seemed no end to Jenny's wet and dragging clothes. Her heavy boned corset angered Clay; it was an implacable weight dragging her under. He broke the strings in back with a savage yank. Only when he felt her slim and vigorous body, sheathed by thin underclothing, swimming easier, did his fear recede.

His shoulder had been badly wrenched. Clay ignored the pain. They might have floated easily in calm water; the storm-whipped river hurled water over them, tossed them, held them helpless in the sucking current.

The blue-white glare of lightning placed them far out in the wide river. Clay could have made the bank himself, even with the injured shoulder, but he doubted Jenny Cockburn's strength to swim that far. Her movements, brushing against him, seemed slower, increasingly weary. Water kept driving into her face, so that she choked and gasped.

Clay thought he saw a crimson glow upriver. That would be fire gnawing at the wreck. Helpless cries still pushed through the storm. They sounded far off and unreal. Clay tried not to think of others fighting to live in the muddy current. If he saved Jenny Cockburn, he'd be lucky.

A flare of lightning as Clay lifted on a wave revealed a white object near them. He called to Jenny. "I think there's driftwood over here! Try to swim to it!"

Jenny made the effort. Clay helped her. They were both exhausted when his hand struck splintered wood. The next lightning revealed a small slab of white-painted superstructure blown off the *Royal Anne*.

They held to the broken edge, floating easier. Jenny's slim figure against his side had the limpness of utter exhaustion. Her long hair washed across Clay's shoulders. He had a bad thought of Jenny, floating lifelessly, with that fine, soft hair washing aimlessly about her face.

"Poor Letty," Jenny said.

"You can't help her by worrying now. Feeling better?"

"I can float like this," Jenny said.

The river had carried them around a bend. The fire on the *Royal Anne* had vanished. The hulk must have gone down. Rain was slackening as the storm moved on.

"Can you try to swim to shore?"

"I'm too tired to swim," Jenny answered wearily. "I swallowed so much water."

The current held them out in the river. After what seemed

like hours later a far, faint flicker of lightning in the south showed the river narrower. Clay guessed they were floating past an island. Below the island they would be in the wide river again. The faint lightning revealed that a whim of the current was taking them closer to the island.

"If you can swim a hundred yards, we'll make the bank," Clay urged.

"I'll try."

Clay had often gambled for large stakes without a rise in pulse beat. When they abandoned that bit of wreckage, fear came again. The river was deep and fast and treacherous, and Jenny was very tired.

He was close when the last of her strength began to go. "Put a hand on my shoulder," Clay panted. Jenny obeyed.

Clay was all but helpless himself, when his foot struck muddy bottom. He staggered upright in water to his shoulders. Jenny tried to stand. The water was too deep. Clay held her up with a quick sweep of his arms.

He gathered Jenny's slender body in both arms and began to wade. She pushed away, and then, as if that were her last strength, went limp, one arm clinging around his neck, her breath coming in gasps. The hard shuddering of her heart thumped against his chest.

Clay carried her to the bank that way, reaching sandy bottom, and then a strip of sloping sandy bank, backed by brush and wild willows. He put her down. They stood exhausted, holding each other. Then Jenny sat heavily on the wet sand. Clay dropped beside her. Jenny's bare arm brushed his arm as she pushed the long, wet hair back from her face. She drew away.

"Well, we made it," Clay said, still breathing hard.

"I'd have drowned," Jenny gulped. Then, stronger: "You won't go aboard the *Kate Sands* now."

"You love him, don't you?" Clay said, staring into the darkness. Out there, bodies were floating downriver. Fine hopes, brave plans, were gone. "You must love him a lot," Clay decided.

"Must I insist that I do?" Jenny said in a low voice.

"He can't help but love you, too. A lucky man. You've many happy years ahead in Virginia, ma'am."

"I hope so."

"A new house where the old house stood," Clay mused. "Stables for fine horses. Men working the fields again. All that, ma'am, and love between you and Captain Cockburn. You've both much to be thankful for."

Jenny sat quietly without replying.

A moment later Clay guessed uncertainly: "You're crying."

"Only a little. I'm tired, and I can't stop thinking about Letty. We . . . we grew up together. She was given to me when we were little girls, and she wouldn't leave after the war. We . . . we belong to each other."

"Ophir Creek, where Letty used to swim," Clay said slowly. "At Ophir Creek Plantation, ma'am?"

"Yes."

"Then your name must have been Jenny Beckford. And Squire Beckford, who didn't get aboard at Oakport, must be your father."

"Yes."

"Did you want him aboard?"

Jenny was quiet for a moment. "No," she admitted. "But I don't want to talk about it or . . . or myself."

Clay dropped the subject. "We'd better stay here until daybreak. There's a risk of water moccasins if we move around. A Memphis-bound boat will pick us up in the morning."

"I can't go on a boat like this," Jenny protested in dismay.

"They'll be rescuing folks in worse shape." He heard Jenny's teeth chattering. "Sit close to me, ma'am. You'll be warmer."

"I'm all right." Jenny said through chattering teeth.

"Since we've almost drowned together, and I've been presented to you as an unwanted husband, there'll be more warmth in common sense than in modesty," Clay said severely.

"I'm not c-cold."

"A rascal, ma'am, can remain a gentleman. A lady is always a lady. And there's small profit in freezing. Sunrise is a long time off."

Jenny stirred toward him, and stopped. Clay reached for her, and, when he felt her shaking with cold, he moved over and drew her close.

"Tuck your legs under," Clay directed calmly. "My mother used to hold me like this, so I know there's warmth in it. She used to sing to me 'Jeannie with the Light Brown Hair' . . . like this. . . ." Clay sang softly, and, before he finished, Jenny had stopped shivering.

"I've heard better voices, ma'am," Clay chuckled apologetically, "but in the late war not an officer in the regiment, or private, either, could sing me down at 'Dixie' on a stormy night. You be the judge."

The calming river murmured at their feet as Clay's "Dixie" lifted to the willow thickets and a few pale stars that were appearing.

Clay ended and cleared his throat. "Pretty bad, I guess, ma'am."

Jenny Cockburn did not answer. She was relaxed in exhausted sleep. Clay held her quietly, listening to the night birds that began to speak and sing in the wild thickets behind them.

Several times in the long hours Clay heard faint, mournful steamboat whistles far upriver. Twice in the night river craft churned upstream, chinks of light, bright red sparks marking the measured thresh of their passing. Clay started to hail the first boat, and then sat quietly.

In the dawn Jenny Cockburn's face looked child-like in the halo of long, fine hair. Her eyes slowly opened. She started at the faint smile close above her face.

"Why didn't you wake me?"

"I'd have been a bigger rascal than I am to deny you sleep, ma'am," Clay said, helping her up. "I'll take a walk and see if anyone lives on this island."

Many of the larger Mississippi islands were farmed. Clay walked along the bank and found no indication this small island was inhabited. Half a mile brought him to the upper end. A dead tree, lodged against the bank, had raked drifting wreckage from the hurrying current. Clay climbed out on the tree and found treasure.

The water yielded a pair of dirty overalls, a white silk evening gown, a blue and yellow bedspread. A soggy cardboard box against the bank contained a gentleman's tall hat and a lady's bonnet with a dripping ostrich feather.

Clay chuckled at the hat and tried on the overalls. They were small, but he could wear them. The tall hat was not a bad fit. Whistling, he hastened back to Jenny Cockburn, and he called before he reached her. "The latest Paris fashions, ma'am! You'll be rescued in style!"

Jenny had braided her hair and scrubbed her cheeks with river water. They were glowing. She stared at the high hat and overalls and began to laugh. When she held up the evening gown and the limp ostrich feather, her amusement grew. But she was grateful, too, for something to wear.

"Breakfast," promised Clay as he retreated again, "will be

served on the first passing boat."

When Jenny called him back, she was wearing the damp dress. Ruefully she said: "The lady who owned it weighed more than I do."

"And wishes, no doubt, she could look like you do, ma'am," Clay said. He held the plug hat in both hands and admired her. "Like a bride," he decided gallantly.

A shadow came on Jenny's face. All the unpleasantness of Colonel Bellinger's accusations dropped between them.

Clay smiled ruefully. "Even a rascal can have his opinion, ma'am."

"You meant to kill him on the *Kate Sands*," Jenny accused.

"I didn't say so."

"If he's waiting in Memphis, you'll try to kill him."

"Why should I?"

"Because," said Jenny, "there can't be two Captain Cockburns." She pleaded: "Can't you go on to Saint Louis? You two needn't meet."

Clay shook his head. "I'll apologize to Captain Cockburn for the unfortunate coincidences which reflected on his good name and embarrassed his wife. You'll not deny me the plea-sure?"

"You mean to kill him," Jenny whispered, her eyes dark with misery. "You can't give me your gentleman's word you don't intend to kill him."

Clay bowed, smiling once more. "By your own word, ma'am, I'm a river gambler and a rascal. My gentleman's word can have little value."

"You're evading. I'll take your word."

Clay looked at her, smiling. His gaze was past her, and he said: "Steamboat smoke coming up the river."

They were picked up by the *Lucius Finch*, a small, shabby

stern-wheeler in the trade between Memphis and the Arkansas tributaries. The steamboat nosed in, and the stage dropped on the sand at their feet. Clay helped Jenny Cockburn aboard in her damp, stained, white evening gown.

A fat, whiskered captain called down in a wheezy voice from the hurricane deck: "Any more off the *Royal Anne* on this island?"

"Not that I know of, Captain."

"We picked up three niggers and a couple of deck passengers downriver. Found several bodies in eddies since daybreak. Bring the lady up and we'll do our best at comfort."

The fat captain was named McWhorter. Bluff, gruff, kindly, he questioned Clay about the wreck and stated with luck he'd have them ashore at Memphis by dark. McWhorter assigned a Negro girl to assist Jenny, and ordered coffee and hot breakfast to her stateroom. He found Clay trousers and a clean shirt, and regretted lacking shoes to fit him and a clean dress for young Mrs. Cockburn.

The shabby little *Lucius Finch* pushed into the stretch of river where the *Royal Anne* had met disaster. A patch of the wreck showed above water, far out from the forested riverbanks.

A small steamboat lingered at the spot. Rowboats were tied to the wreck. McWhorter stopped the *Lucius Finch* close to the other steamboat and was told that passengers saved from the *Royal Anne*, and bodies, were being rushed to Memphis by other steamboats. Both banks had been searched for miles downriver. Captain Siler was known to be dead.

Jenny Cockburn, her fine gown now dry, her hair pinned up once more, stood beside Clay at the deck rail. Clay relayed her question across the muddy current.

The other captain could not say whether a Negro maid named Letty had been rescued. Many Negroes had been taken aboard the *Cherokee*, which had steamed full speed for Memphis.

"Worrying won't help," Clay urged Jenny again. "You'd best rest."

Sundown was fading over the river when the high Memphis bluffs appeared ahead. Most of the day Clay had paced slowly, or sat thoughtfully watching the passing riverbanks. He had not invited company. But now, when Jenny Cockburn appeared on deck, Clay joined her, smiling easily.

"It's all over, ma'am. We probably sha'n't meet again. A pity the trip wasn't longer."

Jenny's slight shrug was almost imperceptible. She looked tired, as if she had not rested during the day.

"Virginia will be beautiful this fall, and more beautiful next spring," Clay mused. "I wish I could see it with you, ma'am, from the new plantation house. You'll be building, I suppose, under the same elms and maples, where the lawns fall away to the river?"

Jenny turned abruptly, staring wide-eyed at him. She gulped. "Good bye, Mister Rivers." Her retreat inside was almost flight.

The *Lucius Finch* used the last light to make her landing among the close-tied steamboats. Great piles of freight were stacked along the shore. Negroes, crew members, passengers, townspeople, moved about on the levee.

A brash young reporter starting aboard tried to speak about the *Royal Anne*. Clay brushed past, barefooted, and strode through the freight piles until he found a carriage for hire.

The driver eyed the bare feet dubiously. "I'm off the *Royal Anne*," Clay said, and that was enough. All Memphis knew by now about the disaster. Clay said: "Wait here." He stood by the carriage, looking down the levee slope.

Jenny Cockburn was one of the last off the *Lucius Finch*. She paused, looking about, and, higher up the levee, she stopped again, a lonely, waiting figure.

Clay walked down to her and gravely asked: "Captain Cockburn didn't come?"

"He couldn't know I'd arrive on this boat." Jenny sounded defiant and near tears.

"If my wife had been on the *Royal Anne*, I'd be meeting all boats."

"I didn't tell him what boat I'd take."

"It's night. You've no money," Clay said quietly. "What hotel shall I take you to? The Gayoso? It's one of the best."

He thought she meant to refuse, then in a small voice she said: "Please."

The carriage was bumping up the rough slope when a cry came from darker shadows beside a mound of freight: "Miss Jenny! Don' go from Letty, Miss Jenny!"

Clay's order stopped the carriage. The two girls, maid and mistress, held each other on the carriage seat, Letty half hysterical with joy, Jenny laughing, too, and close to tears.

A masculine voice called near the pile of freight: "Letty! Where are you?"

"Dat Mister Bob!" Letty gulped. "Mister Phillip an' de Squire come to Memphis, too, lookin' fo' us, an' dey finded me!"

"I don't want to see them now!" Jenny exclaimed in alarm.

"You, there, in the carriage! Jenny! Is that you?"

"Driver, whip those horses!" Jenny urged.

"Jenny! Jenny Beckford!"

Looking back, Clay saw the man break into a run after the

carriage. Farther down the levee two other shadowy figures began to run.

"Faster, driver!" Clay ordered.

The lurching, bouncing carriage whirled up over the Memphis bluff and left the Beckford men behind.

Clay spoke to the colored girl: "They meant to question the captain of the *Lucius Finch* about Miss Jenny?"

"Yas, suh," Letty admitted. " 'Bout Miss Jenny an' you, suh."

"You didn't happen to let those Beckford men think I was Captain Cockburn, did you?" Clay guessed.

"Jes' kind of, a little," Letty admitted reluctantly. "Dey was so mad, Miss Jenny. Talkin' 'bout shootin' Cap'n Cockburn."

"Oh, Letty!"

"It seems," said Clay with amusement, "I'm to be your husband, ma'am, in spite of ourselves. With the added pleasure of being shot for it."

"I don't want anyone killed," Jenny wailed under her breath.

"You didn't, by chance, want the Beckford men to think I was Captain Cockburn when you stood beside me yesterday on the boat, so they could see us from the Oakport bluff?" Clay suggested.

Jenny was silent.

"Why should they want to shoot your husband, ma'am?"

"They don't approve of him."

"I heard of the drinking, dueling Beckford clan of Ophir Creek," Clay said. "A proud and dangerous lot to a man they don't want in the family."

"I don't care to talk about it."

"They'll look for you at the Gayoso House."

"Then I don't want to go there."

Clay considered. "If you care to trust me, ma'am, I know a woman who owns a respectable rooming house. You'll be quite safe and private."

"I'll go there," Jenny decided.

Windows were lighted in the brick house on Third Street where the carriage brought them. Clay told the driver to wait. He pulled the doorbell and said: "Missus Mickle is a plain-spoken widow. You'll find her bark is worse than her bite."

The door opened with an unfriendly jerk. The small, spare woman who looked out from a dimly lighted hallway snapped: "No rooms to rent!"

She caught the door she was closing and looked out again at Clay's broad smile. "Clay Rivers! Drat my hide! I thought it was some fancy drunks! They're always bothering me." Mrs. Mickle looked at Clay's feet. "Great shakes! No shoes!"

"We were on the *Royal Anne* and blown overboard," Clay explained.

Mrs. Mickle reached a quick arm to Jenny. "Why, you poor dear! Why didn't you say so, Clay Rivers? Bring her back to my sewing room, where she can rest."

In the quiet sewing room Clay said: "I've business with Lundy Coughlin. If anyone comes asking for Missus Cockburn or her maid, you have no knowledge of them."

"Knowledge or not, they'll not get in unless she says so," Mrs. Mickle promised tartly. "Clay, she's just a child! And beautiful."

Jenny was smiling, moist-eyed, as she surrendered to Mrs. Mickle's motherly care.

Clay laughed as he turned to leave. "You'll find her quite a grown-up lady, with a will of her own."

★ ★ ★ ★ ★

Lundy Coughlin's Cotton Bale was a landmark on the Mississippi, frequented by gentleman planters, the more sporty element of businessmen and politicians, and aristocracy of the river crews. Lundy's private rooms upstairs were finished with mahogany, rosewood, ebony, rich with silk tapestry and Oriental rugs, lavish in silver, gold, and expensive crystal. Clay looked around with smiling interest.

"All you need now, Lundy, is a harem to fill this nest."

"I'll take diamonds. They've got the beauty an' don't need pampering." Lundy chuckled until his paunch shook. "I used to dream about a fancy place like this while we panned gold in the Sierras. Now I sleep on silk sheets an' dream about that old log cabin you an' me an' Andy Ryan shared. Say, Andy'll be surprised! He's in town. Meant to go back to Saint Louis in the morning."

"Good," Clay said. "Send for Andy, will you? And, Lundy, I need money and clothes within an hour."

Lundy slid back a wall panel, opened a safe, and gestured grandly. "Help yourself. I'll send for Solomon Goldman, a friend of mine. He'll open up his store and dress you quick and proper."

"One more thing, Lundy. There should be a man in Memphis who looks much like me. I want him located as soon as possible."

Lundy stepped to a row of speaking tubes in the wall, signaled the other end, and gruffly ordered through the tube: "Send up Red, Limpy, the Deacon, and Smiley Harris. And tell Sol Goldman I need him quick."

Lundy admitted the four men he had summoned and pointed to Clay. "Take a good look. There's a man in town who looks like him. Find him."

"He arrived on the *Kate Sands*," Clay said. "May call himself Captain George Cockburn."

They looked at Clay carefully, and filed out.

"If he's in town, they'll find him," Lundy said confidently.

Sol Goldman, small and smiling, was making hasty notes of Clay's clothing needs when Andy Ryan burst in. Andy was older than Clay, with broad shoulders, a shock of black curly hair, and zest and vigor for living that never slacked off.

"Been expecting you North for two weeks," Andy stated. "Any luck in that business you wrote about?"

"Tell you later."

"Don't worry about Sol," Lundy said. "He don't talk."

"Forty-four," Sol Goldman muttered, writing. "I don't hear nothing. My ears are bad, shentlemen."

"Lundy, did Andy tell you about the fellow who's been impersonating me?" Clay asked.

"No," said Lundy, interested.

"A couple of years ago, in New York, my baggage vanished," Clay said. "Last winter I met two gentlemen within a month who swore I was very like a Captain Cockburn of Virginia, for whom they'd cashed bank drafts which were not honored."

Sol Goldman shook his head and clucked disapprovingly.

"Clay Rivers could laugh at that," Lundy said.

"Unfortunately," said Clay, "in my lost baggage were papers and letters covering the past life of Captain Cockburn. I took the name of Rivers, Lundy, when I went to California."

Lundy grunted his understanding. "You wasn't the only one."

"I'd never dirtied the family name," Clay stated. "And here was a stranger doing it for me. In the grand style, too. I could almost envy his impersonation. He played Captain Cockburn of Virginia better than I could myself. In New Orleans this trip I heard that a Captain Cockburn had been in town recently, gambling heavily, and had announced he was going to Natchez. I wrote Andy I meant to follow the sign until I found the fellow.

"At Natchez," Clay continued, "I found my Captain Cockburn had left for Montgomery. There was no trace of him in Montgomery. I backtracked, and heard he'd been seen accompanying a planter named Gentry, whose plantation was east of Gainesville, on Ophir Creek. I'd had luck with cards along the way, and I bought a horse, put the money in saddlebags, and rode north toward Gainesville. Unfortunately, at a tavern along the way, I hired a room under my proper name of Cockburn."

"And had another bank draft to honor with the money you were carrying?" Lundy chuckled.

"Somewhat more serious. I was accused of running away with a young lady and stealing gold from her father besides."

"Vat a man!" blurted Sol Goldman between Clay's legs, where he was measuring a seam. "Vas she beautiful?"

"Too beautiful to be true, Mister Goldman," Clay replied. "And there I was with the name of Cockburn, resembling the man, and gold in my saddlebags."

Lundy Coughlin roared with laughter. Even Andy laughed. Lundy demanded: "Not even her pretty arms for a little consolation!"

"I had her brother's revolver muzzle in my stomach, instead," Clay said wryly. "It seems her male relatives were scouring the roads like wild men, planning to shoot Captain Cockburn. I got the story while her brother tried to make me admit where I'd planned to meet her."

"In the other Cockburn's arms somewhere, while they shot you like a dog!" Lundy cried happily. "Oh, to've seen it!"

"Laugh, you mustached hyena," Clay invited. "It wasn't funny. The Gentry Plantation, I gathered, adjoined Squire

Beckford's Ophir Creek Plantation. Captain Cockburn had met Miss Jenny Beckford on horseback rides that had been more frequent than anyone realized. He'd told her all about Fairhill, the ruined Cockburn Plantation in Virginia, and how he'd gone to California after the war, and wandered ever since. I couldn't have been more truthful and convincing myself about myself."

Sol Goldman sighed dreamily. "She fell in loff vith you . . . vith him . . . vith . . . vith. . . ."

"With love," Clay said. "And she urged him to go home and make Fairhill all it had been before the war. He didn't have the heart to go alone or the money to rebuild Fairhill, it seems. Miss Beckford had money from a farm she'd inherited. A day her father was away she left a letter explaining that Captain Cockburn had taken her money from her father's strongbox, and they would be married and settle in Virginia. She went off visiting in one direction. Cockburn departed in another direction. Her letter explained they planned to meet and be married. She evidently didn't suspect that Captain Cockburn had taken her father's money, too."

"I'd have traded the Cotton Bale," Lundy said weakly, "to hear you trying to explain, with that gun against your belly!"

"I was more interested in where the fellow had probably gone," Clay said. "At any moment I expected half a dozen more Beckfords. It seemed easier and safer to take the brother's gun away and leave him asleep in my tavern room, with a sore head. I dropped my saddlebags out the back window and followed them. The tavern barn had a better horse than my tired one, so I borrowed it and rode south. The shortest way out of the state was west, at the river. I turned that way in the night, toward Oakport Landing, and had little doubt the Beckford men were not far behind." Clay's smile had an edge. "They were. I was just out in the river on the

Royal Anne when the Beckfords rode to the Oakport bluff."

Lundy wiped his eyes. "Clay, if this rascal who looks like you is in Memphis, then the girl must be here, too. Shoot the scoundrel and take his place. You'll have a ready-made bride. She'll probably never know the difference."

Clay's look pinched off Lundy's ribald humor. "I've other plans if I can find him," he said slowly.

Within the hour Sol Goldman was helping Clay into new linen, well-fitting gray broadcloth, and soft shoes that might have been made for him.

Lundy answered one of the speaking tubes. When he turned, Lundy's teeth were showing in satisfaction under the big mustaches. "Your man is drinking and gambling at Gil Braxton's Palace Saloon," Lundy announced.

Andy Ryan got to his feet and silently offered a short-barreled revolver. Clay took it, and turned to Lundy's open safe and filled his pockets with money.

"I'll do this alone," Clay said soberly. The look on his face stopped any arguments.

Gil Braxton's Palace was a crowded and noisy place. Clay stopped at the long bar, and men glanced at his fine clothes and bearing, and at his somber face. He had one small whisky, thoughtfully, while he looked about the place, and then he strolled leisurely to the card tables. The man was there in a five-chair game, watched by a handful of spectators.

He was a lean, rather handsome fellow, Clay noted critically, black-haired, clean-shaven, dressed in style and taste. Intently Clay catalogued the features Jenny Beckford loved. Cheek bones rather high, quite like the Cockburn men, a thin nose, a good chin, long, sensitive fingers.

He was not a Cockburn, but perhaps he could have been.

A bit too much the gentleman, though, a shade too swaggering, drinking too much, his laughter too bold.

A player pushed back his chair. "I've had enough. Anyone want my place?"

"If the gentlemen won't mind," Clay said, stepping to the table.

They were carelessly agreeable as he sat down. The saturnine player, gathering the cards at Clay's left, looked at Jenny's man and then at Clay. "Excuse me. Are you two brothers?"

"I'm Clay Rivers, from Saint Louis," Clay said, smiling.

"You ain't, then. This is Captain Cockburn, from Virginia. Your deal, sir."

"I've had the pleasure of hearing Captain Cockburn's name," Clay remarked, shuffling the cards. "On the James River, Fairhill Plantation, isn't it, Captain?"

He looked like a lean wolf at sudden bay, eyes intent, body taut. Clay's glance watched the sensitive hands, quite still now on the tabletop. One hand would have to move to reach a weapon.

Cockburn slowly picked up a white poker chip and tapped it once, and then again. Clay shuffled the cards with a soft, ripping sound. He waited, smiling, for an answer.

"Fairhill is right," the man answered. A damp sheen had come on his forehead, and his decision was abrupt. "I think I'll cash in, too."

"I'll resent it, Captain," Clay suggested, still smiling. "Your absence now would reflect on my presence in the game."

Cockburn's glance glazed and moved past Clay. Clay followed the look over his shoulder. Lundy Coughlin and Andrew Ryan had trailed him and stood impatiently behind his chair, eying the captain across the table.

Clay shuffled the cards. "Well, Captain?"

"I'll lose what I have. It isn't much," was the slightly sullen reply.

"I may bring you luck," Clay suggested, smiling, and he dealt.

Seven spectators had been watching the game when Clay sat down. An hour later men stood three deep around the table, watching fast and reckless poker that would be talked about up and down the river.

Clay bet at random, recklessly, usually losing. His pockets were stuffed with money, and he lost like a gentleman, smiling, unruffled.

Cockburn's sullen playing moved to disbelief, then to flushed elation. Any man, however trapped, could understand chips and gold and banknotes heaping higher before him. Cockburn called for whisky, and continued to win.

"Lundy," Clay said finally over his shoulder, "I'll need more money."

Lundy and Andy emptied their pockets. Business at the bar was all but at a standstill as the game went on. Clay lost steadily. Gil Braxton, a tall man with sideburns, brought money from his safe when Lundy Coughlin spoke to him. Clay lost that, and finally, pushing back his chair, said, smiling: "I see I'll have no luck tonight. Thank you, gentlemen."

Lundy and Andrew Ryan followed him. "I won't say anything," Lundy said disgustedly, jerking a mustache end, "but I thought you aimed to kill him."

"It seems I'm to have guardians tonight, whether I like it or not," Clay commented as they passed outside to the dimly lighted walk. A waiting hack driver called. Clay lifted a finger for the man to wait. "You two can help me if you will," Clay decided.

★ ★ ★ ★ ★

When his friends were gone, Clay stood pensively beside the hack, until Gil Braxton's swinging doors let out the tall figure of Captain Cockburn. The man stopped, not too surprised, Clay guessed. Cockburn had evidently thought about what might happen outside, and what he would do.

In one small thing Clay misjudged his man. Liar, thief, imposter, this imitation Cockburn might be, but not a coward. Perhaps he'd played the fine gentleman enough to have the habit. Or nature, perhaps, had balanced his defects with a certain bravery.

Cockburn stopped, a hand in his right cost pocket, where the bulge of a gun pointed true.

"Don't do that," Clay said calmly. "I mean you no harm." He had not really thought the man would shoot.

A burst of flame through the coat pocket changed all that. The loud report seemed to punch a hot blow against Clay's left arm at heart level. Jenny had been right, of course. There could not be two Captain Cockburns. This one, quite successful at it, his pockets fat with money, had evidently made the decision before he stepped outside.

A second shot caught Clay pivoting and going back a step. The bullet tugged through the front of his coat into the polished side panel of the hack. By then Clay held the short-barreled, heavy-calibered gun Andrew Ryan had silently handed him.

Clay forced himself to face a third shot. His deliberate movement must have been disconcerting. Cockburn's third shot lagged a breath, as Clay fired, and then it was dangerously late by the fragment of a second. Cockburn's coat pocket burst, spilling out the hidden gun. Blood surged darkly on the damaged hand that jerked free. Clay held back the next shot and went forward.

The fellow was backing helplessly when Clay struck him with the short gun.

Alarm had lifted inside the Palace and along the street. "Driver, hold that carriage!" Clay called. He caught the sagging figure and propelled it, sprawling, onto the carriage seat.

"A hundred dollars if you get us away from here!" Clay snapped, scrambling in. "Make for the levee, and circle back on the dark streets."

Clay realized his own arm was bleeding. The first shock had passed, and pain crawled up the arm. His companion stirred. Clay prodded with the revolver.

Cockburn groaned. "I knew you'd try to get that money back!"

Clay helped him sit up in the lurching hack and spoke carefully and coldly: "I'm just in from Oakport Landing. The Beckford men are here in Memphis. Do you understand? They're here to shoot you. Wrap a handkerchief around that hand."

"So you know all about that?" Cockburn muttered as he wrapped the bleeding hand.

"I've been following you from New Orleans. One of the Beckford men mistook me for you. I got away from him and came up the river on the *Royal Anne* with Miss Jenny Beckford. I'm quite aware of everything. You'll come with me," Clay said.

Windows were still lighted in the house on Third Street. Mrs. Mickle opened her door and exclaimed: "I knew you'd be back dressed . . . !" Mrs. Mickle broke off. "Drat it, Clay Rivers! Am I seeing two of you?"

"This is Captain Cockburn, come to comfort young Missus Cockburn."

"Sakes alive! It's high time! She's been real mournful.

Come in." Mrs. Mickle called up the stairs, "Clay Rivers is here!" She turned and winked. "Won't she be surprised at who else is here?" And with satisfaction Mrs. Mickle said: "My daughter's clothes fit her. She's twice as pretty dressed fresh and neat."

Cockburn's bloody hand was hidden in his pocket and so was the hand of Clay's wounded arm. They stood there, wary of each other's movements. Despite his pallor, Cockburn had recovered a trace of swagger.

Jenny saw them both. She stopped and reached to the dark, varnished banister. In pale green, her copper-gold hair combed and pinned up, she was, Clay thought, utterly lovely. His smile, he hoped, showed the pleasure he should be feeling.

"I located Captain Cockburn," Clay said. "He was greatly upset, ma'am, at hearing all you've been through."

Jenny said: "Was he?" She seemed to speak with difficulty, and she held the banister tightly as Cockburn moved to the stairs.

Mrs. Mickle beamed at them, and Clay said: "Captain Cockburn has been uncommonly lucky at cards tonight. He won enough money, I'm sure, to start a new and prosperous life at Fairhill. All that you'd planned to have, ma'am. Eh, Captain?"

Cockburn's surprised agreement was laced with relief and the slightest humor: "More than enough money, Jenny. Aren't you coming down?"

"Who lost the money?" Jenny asked, and once more her words seemed difficult.

"There were five players in the game," Clay answered amiably.

"Were you in the game, Mister Rivers?"

"For a time, ma'am," Clay reluctantly admitted.

"I thought so," Jenny said, stiff-lipped. "I've changed my mind about going to Virginia and rebuilding any plantation."

"Your duty, of course, is with your husband, ma'am," Clay reminded coldly.

"He's not my husband," Jenny denied. "I did have some such thought, and wore my mother's wedding ring, and traveled as a married woman for convenience."

"Land sakes!" Mrs. Mickle exclaimed. "No husband. The poor dear!"

Someone knocked. Mrs. Mickle opened the door. Lundy Coughlin and Andrew Ryan had a third man between them, a thin, severe gentleman with a small Bible in his hand.

"This is the best I could do quick, Clay," Lundy apologized. "He's Preacher Fenn, who don't have no church, but he gives out powerful on a street corner."

"Come in, sir," Clay invited, and he turned to the stairway. "I suspected you'd want a preacher, ma'am. Here he is. You'll have no further worry."

Jenny's reply blazed in protesting anger: "I won't marry anyone!"

"This," the Reverend Fenn protested uneasily, "is most unusual. I was invited here to unite two loving hearts."

"Loving fiddlesticks!" Mrs. Mickle said in exasperation. "Clay, she dressed up in my Susan's Sunday best for someone. A woman can tell."

"I won't listen to any more," Jenny protested indignantly. She gathered up her skirt and ran back up the stairs.

Andrew Ryan cleared his throat in the uncertain silence and kicked a leather traveling case he had brought in. "Braxton helped me locate this man's hotel room, Clay. I paid his account, like you suggested, and brought his baggage here."

"I'll have my papers now," Clay said.

Lundy grunted pleasurably when Cockburn's injured hand came out of the coat pocket in clumsy effort to open and search the leather case.

Clay looked through the small packet that was handed him. He nodded, and put the letters and papers inside his coat.

"I don't know how much you stole from the Beckfords," Clay said. "Empty your pockets. I'll see that they're reimbursed. Take it, Lundy. Let him keep enough to get out of Memphis."

Mrs. Mickle had hurried up the stairs. Clay watched the man fasten his case and straighten sullenly.

"It seems I was mistaken in some things," Clay said slowly. "And now I'll have my name back. I'm speaking to you as Captain George Cockburn. If you use my name again, I'll finish what I should have done tonight. Get going."

Lundy slammed the door after the fellow. The Reverend Fenn edged toward the door, his mouth thin with disapproval. "I see, gentlemen, my services are not needed."

Mrs. Mickle called down the stairway in exasperation: "Clay Rivers, if you've a grain of sense, you'll come up here!"

Clay looked at Andrew Ryan. Andrew smiled, and studied the ceiling, no help at all.

"Wait here," Clay said uncertainly to the Reverend Fenn. He went almost unwillingly and fearfully to the stairs and started up.

Behind him he heard Lundy say: "Forget the door, Preacher. You're in the right place. Just set a while with your Bible."

Mrs. Mickle waited in the upper hall, hands folded under her apron. "She's in there," said Mrs. Mickle, nodding at a door.

Clay swallowed. "Crying?"

"Land sakes! Mad as a wet pullet, I promise you."

"She has a temper," Clay agreed. He knocked uncertainly on the door. "Missus Cockburn . . . Jenny Beckford. Please, I . . . I want to talk to you."

"Drat it!" said Mrs. Mickle. "Sound like a man in love."

Clay's face felt red. He had an idea he was perspiring as he tried to smile. "How should a man in love sound, Missus Mickle?"

"Like a lion roaring gently!" said Mrs. Mickle tartly. "Here's a key. Unlock the door and walk in so she can see you. Maybe that will help."

Clay took the key. "Missus Mickle, I hope you're right."

"I'm a woman, ain't I?" Mrs. Mickle challenged. "And a woman's always right."

"Jenny Beckford," Clay called, "I'm coming in, even . . . even if you scream!"

The Reverend Fenn's remonstrance reached up the stairway: "Gentlemen, I won't be a party to such violence."

Lundy's booming reply lacked sympathy: "Sit down, Preacher. You're still in the right pew. It won't take long now."

Clay devoutly hoped Lundy was right as he unlocked the door and walked in.

Jenny, backed against a marble-topped bureau across the room, ordered in tight anger: "Get out, Mister Rivers!"

Clay had to clear his throat again before he could speak. "You know I'm George Cockburn, ma'am?"

"Yes," Jenny said coldly. "I was sure of it finally on the *Lucius Finch*, when you spoke of rebuilding Fairhill house under the same elms and maples. But I refuse to believe Captain Cockburn, of Fairhill, would force himself into my room like this."

Clay took another breath. "Jenny, will you go to Fairhill with me?"

"No!"

"The same elms and maples and the lawns running down to the river," Clay said. "A new house, Jenny, built as you wish. New fences and clean fields and fine horses. Anything you want in your house."

"I had all that at Ophir Creek, Captain Cockburn," Jenny said coldly. "It will be there when I'm back."

"You were willing to go to Fairhill once."

"Not for a fine house."

"I'll be there, too," Clay said rather desperately. He had crossed the room, talking, and Jenny, pale and sounding stifled, warned: "Don't touch me, George Cockburn."

He had held her in the river, and on the island, the long night through, but it had not been like this, Jenny trembling as he took her close.

"I'm still a rascal, it seems, and this time I'll have my wife," Clay said, stifled, too. "Missus Cockburn, you may scream if you object."

So Wild, So Free

The story that follows was the last fiction T. T. Flynn wrote. It was first published in the anthology, *The First Five Star Western Corral* (Five Star Westerns, 2000) edited by Jon Tuska and Vicki Piekarski. The author never offered this story or his final novel for publication anywhere. The novel, *Night of the Comanche Moon*, was published as a Five Star Western in August, 1995, and is now available in a paperback edition from Leisure Books.

The buggy had been halted by force. The man on horseback by the front wheel was holding the long reins. Kelly saw that much as he looked down the last, long slope to the road.

Any road, Kelly had been thinking as the still-wild black stallion ran tirelessly down through the lower hills and rough breaks, meant ranches, farms, settlements, where good men were bogged in burdens and worries. For Kelly, none of that, ever; he stayed in the mountains and high hills, more free and satisfied than the wild horses he hunted.

It was the buggy top, cut frugally from an old wagon tarp, remembered well, that made Kelly drop his carbine across the pommel as he rode down the brush-dotted slope toward something that was probably none of his business. That he might regret it never occurred to Kelly. His days, and sometimes nights, held zest and few regrets.

His hat had a tilt; a sunburst of gay yellow silk kerchief

draped his neck. His grin was easy and carefree as he halted the stallion so that the carbine muzzle just happened to point at the scowling rider who still held the reins.

"Kelly!" Ruthie Duval's surprised gulp from the sun-cracked buggy seat sounded relieved. "It's years. . . ."

Kelly chuckled. "Almost three years, Ruthie. I move around." Ruthie, he recalled, must be past twenty now, still small-boned, still slender, with a new, surprising maturity on her honest, attractive face. Kelly's glance went to the buggy whip in the road dust—to the thin, red line on the man's jaw and cheek. A Morrison, by the slabby build and pointy face, one of the younger Morrisons, about Ruthie's age. They were a tribe, look-alikes, the Morrisons, clannish and dark-tempered.

Ruthie swallowed with visible effort. "I'll take the reins now, Breck." She was flushed, from temper or fear. A little of both, Kelly decided.

Fight a Morrison and you had to fight them all, sooner or later. They made common cause against outsiders. This one, Breck Morrison, was near-handsome, despite his sharp face. Long brown hair had a vain curl; checkered shirt had a bold look. Cartridge loops were fat on his belt, gun heavy in his holster. And he held stubbornly to the reins, scowling.

Kelly's finger slid to the carbine trigger.

Breck Morrison noted it. His look was venomous as he tossed the reins to Ruthie. "Me 'n' Ruthie were talkin'."

"Talk on." Kelly's smile widened. "I'll wait . . . got all day."

"Some other time!"

The retreating horse drove dust spurts as spurs gouged hard. Kelly frowned over that as he dismounted and picked up the whip. He liked horses. His grin was restored as he returned the whip and settled back in the saddle. "Your buggy stopped much like this, Ruthie?"

"I don't see Breck often," Ruthie evaded. She changed the subject as she gathered the reins. "Kelly, when are you going to stop living like a wild horse, and settle down?"

"I come in." Kelly's eyes were laughing.

"I've heard," Ruthie said. "Drinking, gambling, fighting. . . ."

"Only a little." Memories widened Kelly's grin.

Ruthie's face pinked. "And . . . and saloon girls. . . ."

"Everything you hear."

"Is true, isn't it?" said Ruthie relentlessly. Then she drove on.

Kelly rode easily alongside the creaking wheels. Years ago the buggy had been rickety; it was more so now.

Ruthie said: "I'm almost twenty-two . . . you were five years older. . . ."

Kelly thought back to Ruthie's long braids and crisp bright ribbon bows, to himself lofty with overwhelming age, five years older. His smile was reminiscent.

"I know girls," Ruthie said firmly, "many girls. . . ."

Kelly jested: "So do I."

"Not that kind! Earnest, Christian, home-loving girls, who could do a lot with you, Kelly."

Kelly almost shuddered. "How," he inquired hastily, "are little Johnny and Uncle Tobe?"

Ruthie's face shadowed. "Little Johnny is eighteen now. He . . . he thought everything you did, Mike Kelly, was perfect and wonderful. He still does . . . wants to be like you . . . he's trying hard." Ruthie sounded bitter.

Kelly cleared his throat and tried to adjust to this new Johnny. After all, being Mike Kelly wasn't so bad.

"Rheumatism," Ruthie finished, "has almost crippled

Uncle Tobe. Stop by sometime, Mike, and sit with him."

Gaunt Uncle Tobe, the rock, the pillar—rearing two small kids on the scant ranch land that had been left to them. Kelly had the picture now. This look of full maturity had been forced on Ruthie by work, responsibility, worry.

"Are the Morrisons," Kelly asked mildly, "giving you trouble?"

"No . . . that is. . . ." Worry shadowed Ruthie's face again. "It's Johnny, really. He ordered Breck off our property . . . warned Breck not to speak to me again . . . and did it across Uncle Tobe's shotgun and a buckshot load."

Kelly's grin returned. "Good for Johnny!"

"Wild like you . . . trying to be like you, Kelly!" Ruthie drew a worried breath. "Did you ever hear of a Morrison who would forget a shotgun threat?"

Kelly hadn't, but passed over the fact. "What did this Breck say when he stopped your buggy back there?"

"Breck wanted to take me to the *fiesta* at the Campas Rancho today. He said he'd take me out from now on, or no one else would. He . . . he hinted that Johnny might get hurt if I didn't keep Johnny out of it."

"This Breck," Kelly said with amusement, "must have it bad. What do you do to a man, Ruthie?" The thought brought his chuckle. "I rode in for the *fiesta* . . . go with me."

Ruthie's quick glance was suspicious. "So you can laugh at Breck . . . and make it worse?" Her shrug denied Kelly that. "I couldn't go, anyway. Pete Radwick sent for me. Another baby today. I promised to help."

"Another?" Kelly was wryly amused. "What do they do with so many?"

"You wouldn't know, Kelly. They love them, of course." Ruthie's clouding concern returned. "Johnny will be at the *fiesta*. So will Breck. Will you watch Johnny?"

"No one ever starts trouble at the *fiesta,*" Kelly reminded airily. "But I'll ride herd on Johnny. Don't worry."

Rancho Campas had been an immense Spanish Grant, where proud *dons* had been lavish with hospitality, indifferent of money or business, hot-bloodedly reckless in gambling. Ricardo Campas bore his ancestors no ill will for the vastly shrunken ranch he had inherited. Enough remained for the good life, and some of the traditions, including yearly *fiesta.*

Kelly knew what he would find on the broad, grassy flat beside the green willow thickets along Angel Creek. *Fiesta*—great beef chunks slowly pit-roasting in the old way; deep iron pots simmering fat chili beans; beds of tender shuck corn steaming over hot coals; buckets of fiery red chili, of deceptively cool-looking green chili; hillocks of platter-size tortillas on snowy cloths; steam drifting from huge, smoke-darkened coffee pots—and *fiesta* radiating from the beaming, portly figure of Ricardo Campas, elegant for the day in silvered-studded *charro* clothes, welcoming all.

Kelly arrived with an exuberant flourish, as usual, the burnished black stallion bursting into the lower end of the flat in a skimming run, Kelly's hat tilted, wind-rippling yellow silk folds at his neck, warming laughter on his face.

He called greeting at the long hitch racks and shook many hands on his way to the cook pits and the shifting group around Ricardo Campas.

"¡Miguel . . . *amigo!*" Ricardo's English was better than Kelly's—but this was *fiesta.* Arm around Kelly's shoulder, Ricardo spoke through his graying mustache into Kelly's ear. "Add a hundred to any offer for that big black devil of a horse."

Kelly's chuckle was soft between them. "Took me months

to run him right and corral him. No Spanish jaw-breaker goes into his mouth."

"Two hundred . . . *¡ai!* . . . three hundred," urged the heating blood of earlier *dons,* who had wished and got, at any cost.

"That horse remembers, Ricardo. He'd trample you and take off . . . like he's waiting to do with me."

"*Por Dios* . . . a killer?"

"He could be . . . listen," said Kelly under his breath. "I've been watching a blood-bay stallion, with more mares than this one had. First offer, if I corral him?"

"Sold . . . *now!*" A hasty palm sealed it. "But for the love of every saint, *amigo,* not all my skin to pay."

A good life Kelly had, Kelly thought complacently, as he heaped a tin plate and dropped cross-legged on the grass. That big, blood-bay mustang stallion would take outwitting. But he was as good as corralled, already sold. And what a trip that would be after Ricardo paid. The town would remember Kelly for weeks.

"Gee, Mike . . . Mister Kelly . . . 'member me . . . Johnny Duval?"

Inches taller, shoulders broader. Glancing up, Kelly remembered how it was at eighteen, cocky and confident, juices fermenting. Johnny, Ruthie had said, was like Kelly.

Johnny's gaze admired Kelly's yellow neck silk, Kelly's lank, weathered toughness. "Wish I had a horse'd match that black you rode in," Johnny said enviously. "Need help next time you hunt a bunch?"

"Can't tell." The shiny-eyed admiration was making Kelly uncomfortable. Johnny had a gun belt, a gun—suppose he heard that Ruthie's buggy had been stopped? Breck Morrison was here at the *fiesta,* and other Morrisons. "I'll let you know," Kelly said noncommittally. He sat thoughtfully, absently crumbling a bit of tortilla, after Johnny moved jauntily on.

A half hour later Kelly's face was blank when he confronted Breck Morrison. "If Ruthie Duval is stopped again . . . or Johnny's egged into gunfight . . . I'll track you," Kelly said softly. "Pay heed."

The slabby, near-handsome face turned red. "You makin' threats?"

"Promises," said Kelly coldly. "To you . . . and anyone helps you." He walked away.

Jump one Morrison, you jumped them all. Kelly's grin broke ruefully. He'd ridden in for fun today, and now he was a cat's whisker from a feud, and it would be a mean one. All the Morrisons were vindictive. The thought lurked back in his consciousness as he watched the horse race, another Rancho Campas tradition. To a wagon at the falls of Angel Creek, west to distant cottonwoods, back to the flat—some four miles, all in view of the spectators gathered near the finish rope.

Kelly's black could have won, but four furious miles punished any horse. In the gathered crowd, Kelly watched over thirty riders string dust across the distance, and leaders quirt and spur back to the flat, four almost neck and neck ahead. But Johnny Duval's straining claybank broke the rag-hung finish rope.

Kelly shook his head as Johnny tumbled off to a grinning strut of victory, leading his blowing, lathered horse to Ricardo Campas for the winner's prize—a new revolver with pearl grips. A heady boost for a cocky, wild, young rooster. Not good for Johnny, not good.

There was dancing, as always, on a wide plank floor, put down each year. Kelly was a tireless dancer, but today his mood held him off the floor. Ruthie Duval was on his mind—and Johnny, who wanted to be like Kelly. Ruthie had made it sound accusing—Kelly, roaming the far hills, enjoying life. Girls like Ruthie, Kelly decided, simply couldn't understand. But someone did want to understand. Kelly's roving glance stopped, locked with near and boldly inviting eyes.

He had noticed her honey-colored hair from a distance, her dress cut low, the way she walked—drawing men's eyes even while she looked down discreetly. Kelly drew a breath—and the quick flame fizzled, a sparking moment of promise went soggy. The inviting smile never reached his mouth. Feeling sheepish, Kelly watched the honey hair toss disdainfully as she turned away.

Sundown blazed. Oil flares on tall poles around the dance floor fought back the creeping blue twilight. The first few of waiting fire piles around the flat lifted flames. A scattering of wagons, buggies were leaving. But the guitars, fiddles, laughter, and dancing grew louder, faster. And when, early in the evening, Kelly saw young Breck Morrison loitering near the dance floor, staring off into the night, grinning faintly, Kelly looked that way with interest.

That was how he happened to see Johnny Duval moving from the firelight into the shadows under the willows—and the honey-colored hair at Johnny's side. Trouble, Kelly sensed, but what? He started toward the spot where Johnny had vanished.

Sparks swirled up from the nearest fire as a wood chunk toppled, and the screech that lifted back into the willows sounded like a furious, protesting cat. Music stopped, and the silent tension through which Kelly ran now had an uncertain, explosive quality. Not even his worst forebodings had guessed what happened next. The honey hair fled back into the first firelight in disheveled outrage, the low neck of her clinging dress visibly ripped.

Kelly groaned as he ran. Johnny would never live this down—if Johnny lived. Ahead of Kelly, Breck Morrison was bolting into the willows, gun in hand. No way to stop him.

Back in the willows a gunshot slammed heavily, another gun fired, and the echoes were reverberating as Kelly reached the first low willow branches and black shadows. Twigs, leaves slapped at his face. He lifted a guarding arm—and stumbled over prone legs.

"Johnny?" Swinging back, Kelly thought of Ruthie, who he'd have to tell, who he'd promised to look after Johnny.

"Kill 'im!" called thickly from the ground. "He shot me an' run!"

Not Johnny's voice—but Johnny's trouble. Breck Morrison had been cut down with a bullet. First the girl, then a Morrison. Kelly could have groaned again over Johnny's thinning chances.

"I hope he gut-shot you," Kelly said savagely as suspicions crystallized. Other men were rushing to the spot. "Here's one!" Kelly shouted. Covered by that, he headed out of the willows, trying to think like Johnny would be thinking.

Fiesta had ended in confusion. Outraged women had closed protectively around the honey hair. Kelly ran, unnoticed, toward the long hitch racks. The shadowy, bolting run of a horse faded from the racks ahead of him. When he reined his own horse the same way, ominous, fire-silhouetted figures were running to the racks.

South, the ranch road, and town. North, beyond the black line of willows, Angel Creek scoured against a high cutbank on the other side. Where the willows thinned ahead, wagon ruts dropped into the creek, lifted through a narrow slit in the high bank to open range. Instinct guided Kelly. Johnny was rattled, desperate. North lay fastest escape. The black horse splashed across the shallow creek and topped the high bank. A slash of the rein ends exploded into a tremendous run.

Kelly had no solution for this unholy mess. They might not have hanged Johnny for decently stealing a horse, forgiving youthful error. Shooting a proddy gunman might have been approved. But this: virtue—Kelly snorted—defiled. A righteously indignant Morrison shot down. Kelly groaned, once more. Johnny, strutting his new, thin shell of manhood, had dug a dismaying pit.

Eyes adjusting to the pale starlight, black horse running like a scudding ghost, Kelly thought how this would crush Ruthie. Her burdens, heavy enough, did not deserve this. And Ruthie's eyes would condemn Kelly.

A straight line led quickest away from danger. The line this way was north to the Lone Rock Tank, on to the higher breaks beyond, and twenty-odd miles of dry, lifting hill country to the next water. Dubious safety lay that way for Johnny, and angry men coming behind him, Kelly knew, must be thinking the same thing. He hoped instinct was right —and it was. Off to the left a gun muzzle blossomed red.

"Johnny!" Kelly veered over, shouting again. He saw the shadowy horse and rider slow, and halt. Johnny was peering suspiciously, gun in hand, when Kelly reached him.

"I thought. . . ." Johnny was hoarse.

Kelly swung off. "Swap horses! You'll never get anywhere on that raced-out claybank!"

"I never touched her," Johnny said fiercely, despairingly, as he dismounted. "Sudden-like, she let out a scream an' run from me."

"If you can stay on my horse," Kelly said swiftly, "get to Ruthie and tell her what happened. Then head for the hills. On the west shoulder of Little Baldy, you'll cut a deer trail.

Follow shod tracks to a small pole cabin. Wait there for me."

"That's more'n s-seventy miles. . . ."

"If you make it," Kelly said coldly. "Who is that girl? I never saw her before."

"Rose Ella Bunker. Her old man started a jackleg blacksmith shop in town."

"You'll learn, maybe," Kelly said curtly. "Now get going, if you can sit that horse. I can't stand the sight of you."

He held breath while Johnny stepped up. The edgy black sidled nervously, snorted, then obeyed the reins. Johnny vanished into the night, shaken, stripped of swagger, and, Kelly knew, in real danger.

At Lone Rock Tank, a shallow seep pool, Kelly watered the claybank and left trampled sign, easy to read. Beyond the tank, a cattle trail angled up into the first rough breaks, where tracking was almost impossible on a moonless night. Some two leisurely hours later, Kelly tied the claybank to a dead cedar stump beside a scoured wash, and stretched comfortably on the scanty grass tufts.

Stars dusted the sky. Coyote clamor lifted eerily in the distance, died away, broke out again as Kelly gazed at the sky and thought of Johnny, Ruthie, the Morrisons—and himself. A mess, he decided—and he was sleeping soundly on it, hat over his eyes, when rattling hoofs up the wash brought him standing in full daylight.

A shirt-tail posse that must have waited for dawn at Lone Rock was tracking Johnny's horse at a gallop. The bony, white-mustached old man in the lead, Kelly saw, was Old Rance, first and worst of the Morrison clan.

"He ain't Duval!" Huck Morrison, father of Breck, slabby son of Old Rance, shouted it.

Riding at Old Rance's stirrup was Ed Powers, the deputy

from town, and Kelly relaxed a little. Impartial and friendly, Ed Powers was stubborn only in holding closely to the law.

Kelly's humor drew crinkles at his eyes and bent his mouth as the blowing horses pulled up around him.

Old Rance glared at the claybank. "That 'n's the hoss young Duval rode in the race!"

"My horse now," Kelly said.

"Don't fog around it, feller. Where's the kid?"

Kelly yawned. By now they all knew he'd swapped horses with Johnny, and baited them off into the empty breaks.

"Why ask me?" Kelly said reasonably. "I've been asleep. If you're the law, find him yourself, you back-shooting old fence-cutter."

Huck Morrison erupted angrily: "Drag it outen him at a rope end."

They'd drag him, too, Kelly was aware. Any Morrison would. But Ed Powers spoke sharply from his horse. "Kelly didn't shoot anyone and wasn't near the girl."

"That," Old Rance blared, "ain't the point! He helped Duval git scarce on a fast hoss! Makes him guilty to us! He'll git the same."

"Not here," said Ed Powers with stubborn calm. "I'll take Kelly in . . . no help needed, or advice."

"We c'n wait!" Old Rance was malevolent.

The deputy rode beside Kelly, and spoke under his breath. "You're safer this way." Powers was regretful. "You shouldn't have helped Johnny Duval. That girl business . . . he don't have a friend."

Kelly grinned. "One friend," he reminded, and after a moment Ed Powers grinned, also.

This was to have been Kelly's day in town—one to remember. It still was his day, Kelly reflected wryly as a fast trot brought them in through the hot, gray dust of Main Street. Kelly saw the old buggy with an ancient tarp top waiting in front of the deputy's small office, next door to the saddle shop.

"I'd like to talk to Johnny's sister alone," he told Ed Powers.

"That ain't surprising," Ed drawled. "Well, go ahead."

Ruthie had been sitting listlessly inside the front window of Ed's office. She was on her feet when Kelly stepped in and closed the door.

"Johnny said they'd probably catch you," Ruthie said. She hadn't slept, Kelly guessed. She had a tired sound, a tired look, crushed, as if the burdens, finally, were too much.

He had an urge to comfort her, but there was scant comfort in Johnny's trouble. Kelly's chuckle covered that. "Johnny stayed on my horse and got away . . . that's the important thing."

"Anyway for a time, I suppose," Ruthie said. "But what's ahead for him? Breck's limping around town with Johnny's bullet in his leg and . . . and that girl and her story?"

Ruthie's unhappy eyes said that the blame was Kelly's. It was Kelly who had set the example. And that was the moment that Kelly, being Kelly, was inspired.

"Breck Morrison's in town here . . . able to walk?"

"Yes."

"Mmm-mm . . . Ruthie." They were alone, but Kelly lowered his voice cautiously, humor lighting his face as he spoke rapidly.

Red surged into Ruthie's cheeks; tired worry in her eyes flared into indignation. "You would think of something like that!" she said bitingly. "You and . . . and your saloon girls!"

"If it would help Johnny . . . ?" Kelly held his breath.

"I'd never get over being ashamed." Ruthie's cheeks were

flaming. "Why, I've never. . . ."

Kelly believed that, too, but if Ruthie could bring herself to do it. . . . He patted her small shoulder reassuringly as Ruthie left the office.

Minutes later Ed Powers said: "Sure, I mean to talk to the Bunker girl. Didn't have a chance last night." Ed frowned across the pine table that was his desk. "Breck Morrison watching them and grinning don't mean a thing."

"Ed, when I see a wolf start a stalk, I look where he's looking. She'd already passed me a let's-walk-out look."

"You collect them kind of looks, Kelly. I'll get her story, and Breck Morrison's . . . and they'll tack Johnny Duval's hide high, and salt it. Yours, too, for mixing in."

"Just do like I asked," Kelly urged. He was still inspired, confident.

But when the honey-haired girl walked into the small office, drawing glances even from across the street, Kelly had first doubts. She looked like a church-choir girl now, a bruised flower, still frightened.

"Here, miss," Kelly said, offering the chair by the front window, where Ruthie had been sitting.

The honey-haired girl looked at him appraisingly, Kelly decided. She looked at the window that would display her to all the street, and sat down like a satisfied cat. The dusty, bare little office suddenly seemed full of Rose Ella Bunker, honey hair, clinging dress, and a deal of Rose Ella which came readily to imagination.

Ed Powers looked at her, and drew a breath. *You, too,* Kelly thought, less inspired by the moment. He had not expected Old Rance Morrison to stalk in, trailed by Huck Morrison, Breck's father, or other men to gather in the doorway, inspecting Rose Ella with interest and Kelly with dislike.

Ed Powers closed the door against the curious faces. "You two can stay, I guess," he told the Morrisons. "Breck's coming to give his side of it."

"We got Breck's side . . . a lead slug in his leg!" Old Rance said coldly. "Gal, tell yourn."

Rose Ella faltered. "I'm still so shamed-like. Didn't seem no harm, likely, walking out like that. . . ."

The last of Kelly's inspired confidence slowly faded as Rose Ella Bunker tearfully nailed Johnny's hide barn-roof high and completely salted. Standing beside her chair, looking across her honey hair, Kelly could see through the dusty window to the street, and not even Breck Morrison, emerging from the Yoke Bar across the street, gave much hope.

Breck was using a knob-headed cane, limping painfully, Kelly hoped. He was barbered, slicked up in a new loud shirt and wool pants, and looked, Kelly decided, well pleased with himself.

It won't do, Ruthie! Kelly wanted to open the window and shout warning. *Shouldn't have talked you . . . !*

Kelly stopped thinking. Ruthie's small figure was already running lightly, swiftly from the walk into the street.

"Breck!"

Not a cat screech, like last night, but it carried—it carried, even through door and window into Ed Powers's office, into Rose Ella Bunker's ears. She looked out the window. She stopped talking. She stiffened.

Breck Morrison halted in the street, alarmed, it seemed to Kelly, then stunned as Ruthie wrapped tearfully around him —or so it appeared to Kelly. The town, Kelly guessed, had never seen anything like it on Main Street. Nor had Breck Morrison, anywhere. Rose Ella's frozen look watched through the window.

Kelly himself was fascinated as Breck Morrison's near-handsome head bent down—or Ruthie pulled it down. That kiss—Kelly winced, then was queerly resentful as he waited for it to end. Ruthie didn't have to be so convincing, as if she were blindly enjoying it.

Breck Morrison's enjoyment could not be doubted. His arms closed around Ruthie in full possession—and Rose Ella Bunker hissed like an aroused cat. "After all I done for Breck . . . tricking Johnny Duval that way. . . ."

"Gal," Old Rance shouted, "what's that you're sayin'?"

Rose Ella, shriller by the breath as she watched through the window, said spitefully: "Breck put me up to it last night . . . to even a grudge, he said!"

"Your dress was tore, gal!"

"Breck said I was to do it that way. Seemed like I couldn't deny him."

"Breck!" Old Rance said it like an oath as he yanked the door open and plowed through the men outside, who were looking at the street. Huck Morrison followed. Kelly was at their heels in dark, hard temper, for the first time since he could remember.

Old Rance, white mustache quivering, saved him the trouble. Breck Morrison had unwrapped himself and was grinning hugely, foolishly down at Ruthie when Old Rance's heavy revolver barrel belted him squarely on the side of the head.

Old Rance did not stop to see Ruthie gasp or Breck's staggering fall. "Drag your low-down pup home, Huck, an' keep 'im there!" Old Rance rasped over his shoulder as he kept going. "He's made fools outta us we won't live down."

Kelly caught Ruthie's arm as she started to run toward her buggy. "Johnny's all right now. It worked."

"What about me?" Ruthie said, near tears. "The whole

town watching!" Ruthie was scrubbing her mouth with a handkerchief.

That was the moment, in the dusty street, when Kelly was inspired again. "Forget the town, Ruthie. All you need is a good man to take hold and carry the troubles."

Ruthie looked at him with suspicion. Kelly's grin was spreading. "What man?" Ruthie asked, still suspicious.

Kelly thought fleetingly of the high hills—but he was looking at Ruthie. The empty hills, he thought without regret at all, the empty, lonely hills. He tilted his hat again, because this was the way he suddenly felt. "I'll drive you home and tell you all about him," Kelly said.

Some of Ruthie's suspicion drained away, but she had known Kelly a long time. "I have to stop at the Radwicks' and help with the new baby," Ruthie remembered, watching him.

Kelly's grin held. "I was thinking we ought to," he said—and he had known Ruthie a long time, also. Ruthie was smiling faintly, almost secretively, as she let Kelly help her into the buggy and, following her, take the reins.

Hell's Cañon

T. T. Flynn completed this story on September 1, 1944. He did not give it a title. It was accepted by Popular Publications on October 1, 1944. The author was paid $180.00. It was titled "The Kid from Hell's Canyon" when it was published in *Fifteen Western Tales* (1/45). For its first book appearance, this title has been shortened.

I

"BLUE GOLD BUSHWHACK"

Big Ollie Martin pistol-slugged the unshaven, trail-dirty stranger as impersonally as he would have axed a crippled steer. More so, in fact. Steers carrying Ollie's M-O brand were worth money. A range tramp without guns, horse, or money, who argued with Ollie Martin, was worse than nothing.

Nine men saw the cat-quick explosion of violence in the Curly Horn saloon, one of Ollie's Palomas properties. They saw the stranger fold and drop. Not one of the nine showed open resentment.

Ollie holstered the heavy gun carelessly. He had the look of an outlaw range bull, thick-shouldered, scarred, cunning, challenging.

"Bums learn manners in Palomas," Ollie stated. He spat

on the thin skim of dirty sawdust beside the stranger's limp body, and gave a careless order to the blank-faced barman. "Throw him out the back door, Rip."

Ollie picked up a badly bent and twisted half dollar from the bar. "Put this junk back in his pocket. He c'n spend it anywhere but in one of my places."

That drew grins. Ollie owned or controlled most of the businesses in Palomas.

The half dollar bounced on the bar as Ollie tossed it back. "Dusty, you and the boys ready to ride?" Ollie asked. He walked heavily out the front swinging doors without waiting to see if they were followed.

Three men left their drinks and trailed him out. The bartender walked to the stranger, caught an old sombrero off the floor, seized the limp form by the shoulders, and dragged it out into the gathering dusk.

Two dogs were standing close, sniffing suspiciously, when the stranger sat up groggily. One dog growled as they backed away.

Night was coming on in dirty gray shadows before dark-of-the-moon blackness. A hollow log trough under a wooden pump nearby held water.

The stranger wet the end of a bandanna in the water and gingerly wiped drying blood from the side of his head and in front of his right ear. The scalp had a nasty gash.

His sombrero had been tossed on the ground. He found the bent half dollar in his pocket and lifted his eyebrows in surprise. He stood there in the coming night, a lonely, shabby figure, lean as a saddle string worn by hard use, but still tough.

He had nothing but the mud-stained, dusty clothes he wore, and the coin. He was turning the coin in brown, supple fingers as he limped out to the single main street of Palomas, ankle-deep in brownish dust. He walked like a man whose body was fighting fatigue that was close to drunkenness, greater than his remaining awareness.

Palomas was not a boom town, but neither did it have the feel of emptiness this early in the evening. A few wagons and saddle horses were on the street. Windows were lighted.

The stranger stopped by a restaurant doorway as if an invisible hand had jerked him to a halt. He breathed deeply of the smells of ham, steak, good food.

Nelly's Home Cooking was painted on the window. Several customers looked up from their plates as the stranger walked in and sat at the back end of the counter with a little grunt of relief. He ironed out a wry twist to his lips when his hand strayed to a shirt pocket and found no tobacco sack.

The girl, hurrying back and forth, ignored him through several trips to the kitchen. Business was brisk. Her orders rang briefly, clearly, crisply to the old Chinaman who was doing the cooking.

The stranger watched the light on her brown hair, the smiling changes of expression on her face. He was lost in thought when she suddenly stopped in front of him.

"What'll it be, mister?"

"Depends on how you like my money."

"A bent-up half dollar is as good as any other, I guess," she said. "No matter what Ollie Martin thinks."

"You've been hearing things," the stranger said. He put the damaged coin on the counter.

"News travels fast in a town like this," she said impersonally. She examined the coin. "Bullet hit it?" The stranger nodded, and she dropped the half dollar in her apron pocket. "What'll you eat?"

"Half a dollar's worth of the cheapest grub," he said, and

grinned again. "Make it forty cents' worth, and a sack of tobacco."

She brought him steak and potatoes, carrots, dried apple pie, coffee, a big glass of milk, and a sack of tobacco. Then she went about her duties.

The stranger's hand shook as he caught up the fork. He forced himself to eat slowly. After a little he stopped and rolled a cigarette, and drew deeply, luxuriously on it.

Most of the customers had straggled out by the time he had cleaned the plate and rolled another cigarette. The girl had ignored him. She stopped now, glance level.

"Are you Nelly?" he asked.

"Nelly Boyle."

"Forty cents never bought that much grub in here before, Nelly."

"You never ate in here before," Nelly said, unabashed. "When did you eat last?"

"Three days ago."

Nelly Boyle showed no pity. "And as soon as you hit town, you tried to trade your last money for whisky." She shook her head and regarded him with disapproval. "No wonder you're a bum. Not that I'm excusing Ollie Martin for what he did. You should have had better sense than to talk up to a man like Ollie."

"He just looked like any man to me, ma'am."

"There's horses an' horses, and men an' men," Nelly said briskly. "Ollie's mean. He always was mean. He's got guts and guns and men and money to back it up. Ollie wouldn't bother killing a poor specimen like you, even if you had a gun. But he's mean enough to stamp right on you when he feels like it."

The stranger ruefully touched the side of his head. "He stamps hard, don't he, ma'am?" He stood up. "Thanks for the grub. Maybe someday I can pay back."

"Wait a minute." Nelly took the coin from her pocket. "This was a special piece of money, wasn't it?"

"Sort of."

"I thought so, or you'd have pounded it out flat," said Nelly briskly. "Have you got a horse?"

"No, ma'am."

"Saddle?"

"No, ma'am."

"Guns?"

"No, ma'am."

Nelly shook her head. "Don't be edging away until I get my say," she said impatiently. "Where are you going to sleep tonight?"

"I'll find a place."

"I don't know why I'm doing this," Nelly said bluntly. "You're just about as dirty and sorry a stranger as I've seen. Won't even bother to shave or keep clean. Get yourself washed up and sleep in the little room back of the kitchen tonight. Charley Goon, my cook, used to sleep there, but he moved over with the Chinaman who cooks for Ollie Martin, in the other eating place."

"Do I have to shave, ma'am?"

"You look like a scarecrow now," Nelly said critically. "But if you're too lazy to shave, keep your face sprouted up that way. Just get clean. I can't stand dirt around. What's your name?"

"Yes, ma'am. Folks call me Chance."

"Last Chance," said Nelly. "That just fits you. Last chance to be a man and settle down. The back door to the room will be unlocked. Don't come in drunk tonight, if you find free drinks. There'll be grub in the morning."

"Thank you, ma'am," Chance said meekly.

Nelly looked at him suspiciously. "Your eyes aren't saying what your lips are. You're laughing at me behind that soft talk." Nelly leaned over the counter. "Those riding boots cost top hand money, and they aren't hand-me-downs. You've got a rubbed spot on the side of your pants where you've been wearing a gun holster."

"Last Chance fits me, and so will the back room tonight," Chance said, meeting her look. "That is, if the offer still goes, ma'am."

"Of course," said Nelly. "I can see you're busted and down to walking. I guess you can ride."

"A little."

"Shoot?"

"Medium, I'd say." Chance touched the side of his head, sore and swelling. "Even if I can't duck a gun barrel quick enough."

"A starved man ain't quick at much but eating," said Nelly. "I've seen them in here before. And Ollie Martin doesn't believe in giving warning. When he makes a play, it's over quick, before the other man catches on. That's one reason he stays on top." She drummed on the counter with her fingertips, considering, measuring him. "Wish I could see what was under that raggedy brush on your face," she said, partly to herself. "But your eyes look all right. There's something about your voice that sounds all right."

"Thank you, ma'am."

"Don't go laughing at me again," said Nelly coldly. "This is business, and I'm not laughing about it. Want a riding job out at my ranch?"

"What kind of a ranch, ma'am?"

"A cow ranch," said Nelly curtly. "And don't lift your eyebrows about it. The ranch'll be big again, one of these days, like it used to be. I opened this place to have cash money."

"Your husband runs the ranch, ma'am?"

"My grandfather. Everyone calls him Dad Boyle."

"I'm hired," said Chance promptly.

"Here's your money," Nelly said. "In the morning, I'll stake you to an outfit."

"I'll buy that half dollar back out of my first pay," Chance said. He hesitated. "I set store by it, miss."

Nelly put the twisted piece of money back in her apron pocket without comment. Her blue eyes appraised him with new interest as he limped out.

Dad Boyle was a surprise. The old man stood, crippled and bent, beside a sweating horse at the ranch corral. His left leg was twisted and shorter than the other. His back was twisted, so that he hunched forward, and one guessed that pain was often with him. Perhaps pain put the hostile, searching blaze in his deep old eyes.

"So you're the best Nelly c'n find," Dad Boyle said in a voice close to a snarl. "Sent you out on her own horse. Bet she bought them new gun and rifle an' belt. Whyn't she make you shave?"

"Maybe she'll get around to it," Chance said mildly.

"Git a shovel outta the shed over there an' ride past that crick bend an' the big cottonwood an' foller your nose about four mile, to the first ridge. Couple of the men are waitin' by the bald outcrop of rock you'll find. I got to ride on to town."

Dad Boyle threw himself up on the horse with an explosion of agility that belied his age and damaged body. He rode off fast, hunched forward in the saddle, one stirrup shorter than the other.

An hour later Chance Kimberly was using the shovel near the bald outcrop of rock.

Jimmy Dee, pint-sized, talkative, hunkered at the side of the hole. "Bury him deep, boys. Sam Wilson was a good son-of-a-gun."

Ed Peck, a long and rangy man, said: "Sam makes the third one. We had an idea Sam had run into trouble. But we didn't know where he'd rode off to. Wasn't for the sniff we got downwind, we'd've rode past him today."

"Don't tell me Sam didn't find somethin'," said Jimmy Dee, rolling a cigarette. "Else why was he dry-gulched?"

"Quit talking an' help with the shovel," said Ed Peck.

The dead man had been missing two weeks. Buzzards and coyotes had found him, despite the thicket into which the body had been dragged, the brush that had been thrown over it.

Chance wiped perspiration from his face and walked over to the body. Sam Wilson had been big-boned and powerful. He was not even a dead man now—he had lived and died and nature had taken him back. The nearby prints of Wilson's horse were already vanishing under recent wind and rain.

Chance's intent look noted something of interest. He stooped and worked at what was left of the dead man's clenched left hand. He straightened with a small bit of bright blue-green rock in his own hand. The edges were rough, sharp, as if the fragment had recently been broken off.

"Pretty piece of rock," Chance said, back at the grave. "Ain't any more around here like it."

"Looks like the chunk Dad Boyle's got over his fireplace," said Jimmy Dee. "Dad Boyle says he got it up in Little Bear Cañon fer Miss Nelly, when she was a kid. She liked it so much he always kept it around. Billy Poor, the cook, started to throw it out once, an' Dad Boyle swore he'd take after Billy with a shotgun if the chunk came up missing."

"How'd the old man get in the shape he's in?" Chance asked.

"Made the mistake a long time ago of drivin' some cattle to the railroad over land that Ollie Martin claimed," Ed Peck stated. "Somebody stampeded the drive. Dad Boyle's horse went down, and he got trampled. Put him in a wheel chair for years."

"Go on an' say the rest of it," Jimmy Dee panted as he hoisted out a shovelful of hard earth.

"Ollie Martin chawed away a heap of Dad Boyle's holdings in those years," said Ed Peck. "It ain't left Dad Boyle any too happy about Ollie Martin. Things are set to bust."

"Miss Nelly started cookin' in town an' saved what they got left," Jimmy Dee supplied as he climbed out of the hole. "You c'n dern' near tell who likes Ollie Martin an' who don't. Them that don't, eat with Miss Nelly. She's made a heap of friends."

"You can't stand off Winchesters with fried eggs," said Ed Peck laconically. He clambered awkwardly down into the deepening hole.

"What was Sam Wilson looking for?" Chance asked.

"Fer sign of what happened to two other men. There ain't any doubt Ollie Martin could tell, but try an' prove it. Ollie Martin's on top of the heap."

"A fat bank account never took the meanness out of a man," Chance said. "Not going to wait for the sheriff to see the body?"

"Waste of time," said Jimmy Dee. "Jep Keyes, the sheriff, is a friend of Ollie's. Stuck on Ollie's high-handed, purty daughter, too."

"So Ollie's got a daughter," Chance said after a moment's pause. "Pretty and high-handed, you say? Mean streak like her old man, I guess?"

"I wouldn't say yes or no," said Jimmy Dee. "Ollie's got his own special brand of meanness. Lucille Martin is just high-handed an' cold-blooded. Wants what she wants an' gits it . . . if possible. That there bay horse of Miss Nelly's you're ridin' is the fastest Quarter horse in a week's ride, an' can take circle on range work like any bronc'. Lucille Martin aims to own him. She ain't quit tryin', and won't. She's got no use for Miss Nelly on account of it. But I don't know how mean a trick she'd do Miss Nelly."

"The sheriff takes orders from Ollie Martin, I guess," Chance suggested.

Ed Peck broke in from the grave hole. "Don't count on that. Jep Keyes is vain enough to be his own man. Give Jep proof enough an' I'll bet he'd arrest Ollie, much as he'd hate to do it."

They buried what had been Sam Wilson.

II

"HALF DOLLAR'S WORTH OF HELL"

"I'll ride out and see what the range is like," Chance decided. He grinned. "Where's Little Bear Cañon? I might go after a chunk of that pretty rock, for my little girl . . . if I ever have one."

"Ride south and you'll see Teepee Butte," said Ed Peck. "Bear Creek's the first water beyond. Foller it up an' you're in Big Bear Cañon. Couple of miles up, there's a side cañon. That's Little Bear."

"An' it's Ollie's range over thataway," said Jimmy Dee. "Git your little girl first . . . an' the purty rock later. Iffen you want both."

Chance mounted; his expression, if any, hidden by the brushy, untrimmed stubble on his face.

Teepee Butte was black rock, named to match its shape. Bear Creek was shallow, running narrowly in the wide sands and gravels of the flood bed. The range was rolling, with stunted trees scattered to the limit of sight, and little thickets and bosques near the water, like islands of refuge in the pitiless open.

Big Bear Cañon had flat grazing and thickets along the singing water. In some spots the sides were craggy, forbidding naked rock that sheered toward the sky. In other places the steep cañon slopes were covered with massed trees.

Chance rode easily, a lone and contented-looking figure, not outwardly wary. The cattle he saw looked as if the grazing had been good. A deer broke from a thicket beside the creek and bounded out of sight ahead. Chance's hand made an involuntary twitch toward the new rifle in the new saddle boot Nelly Boyle's money had bought. He grinned slightly in the wild-looking stubble and rolled a cigarette as he rode on.

Little Bear Cañon forked off to the right. It was more narrowly sheer in the side walls. A meager seep of water crept down through a scoured and boulder-clogged bed. Little Bear Cañon was serpentine, cleaving back into the rising mountains with a sharp upslope, not inviting man or beast.

Cattle and shod horses had beaten a rough and narrow trail into the cañon. Chance studied the trail as he rode slowly. The blue-green rock was not here at the mouth, and not in the water-worn boulders and gravel in the run-off channel beside the trail. More horses than cattle had passed in and out of Little Bear Cañon and left the sign to read. A jay screamed ahead from a gnarled tree high up on the precipitous slope.

Chance reined in, listened to the deep quiet, and rode on

slowly, eyes questing intently. The voice that stopped him came from the steep cañon slope to the right.

"Lost your way, stranger?"

The voice was a hundred yards up, where trees and brush and boulders clogged a little bench on the slope. It was clear and cold through the quiet. The speaker himself rose slowly upright into view, rifle held ready. He was bare-headed with a dark mustache, armed and challenging.

"Just looking around, mister," Chance replied.

"Ain't that the Boyle girl's Quarter horse?"

"Might be. Does it make any difference?"

The jay screamed again in the distance. The horse stood quietly. Between Chance's knees the fast and clever little horse seemed to be poised, straining for an order, as if it sensed an unrevealed tension.

"Not much difference," the stranger up the slope said. "Who's with you?"

Chance laughed. "Wait and see," he said. "Might be the sheriff."

Their words had little meaning in the quiet, but the tension filled the little cañon like a string growing tighter, until the slightest touch would make it hum—or break.

"Ride back and get the sheriff," the stranger said. "No hurry, I'll be waiting."

"Wait a little," Chance said. "I'll bring him."

The string of tension was tight to the snapping point as he gathered the reins. The stranger stood, looking down the slope, rifle held loosely. Chance reined Nelly's horse around and swept his hat up in straight-armed salute.

When the hat came down, it slashed fast and hard against the horse's ears and neck, and the spurs rowled hard as Chance yelled shrilly. The plunge of the horse snapped him back in the saddle, but it was the starting jump of a fast

Quarter horse, in full racing stride while most bronchos would still be getting set to run.

Chance leaned forward, spurring, yelling encouragement. The rifle shot came like the snapping of the tight string—as Chance had known it would come, at his back, as Sam Wilson's back had taken a bullet.

He saw rock chips fly off to the right, heard the rifle after him again, and then again. The horse was plunging like falling mountain water down the rough and sharply dropping trail. It was sure-footed, faster than any horse Chance had ever ridden over rough country.

The last bullet passed closely, and a turn of the cañon shielded him. The wider reaches of Big Bear Cañon opened before him, and so did another gun across Big Bear Cañon. Chance saw the second man up the slope across Big Bear Cañon, standing in the open, pumping lead at him. He swung the racing, sure-footed horse toward Teepee Butte and urged it faster.

There were two guards, and each had known he was alone. They had let him ride into Little Bear Cañon to see his purpose, and they had not meant for him to come out. Bullets searched after him with shrill, deadly intent. Chance found himself dreading a hit on the horse. The soaring, gallant rush of the little horse deserved something better than a bullet.

If he was trailed, the men kept back out of sight. Chance guessed they knew the horse could not be caught in this country in an outright run.

The afternoon was waning when Chance rode to the big rambling ranch house that was Ollie Martin's range headquarters. There was another house in town, but here Ollie had started, and here he preferred to stay most of the time.

Once more Chance was weary. One night's sleep, two

good meals, had not been enough to make a new man of him. He straightened, however, eyes intent on the girl who walked out of the long adobe house.

There were corrals, two windmills, outbuildings beyond the house. A ridge to the northwest was a good break against the winter storms. Tall trees had been left growing and others had been planted long years ago and tended, so that even nature seemed to be rooted firmly around Ollie Martin's success. It was the girl Chance watched as he swung down.

She was tall and free-striding, with golden hair coiled over her ears. *Pretty,* Chance thought, *but not soft.*

She greeted him with blunt purpose. "Did you bring that horse here to sell?"

"I came here to see Ollie Martin," Chance said. "The horse ain't for sale." Chance added: "Or have you heard?"

She nodded. She was looking at him and not the horse. Her eyes were blue, not hard, not soft. "You can tell me," she said. "I'm his daughter."

"I happened on some of your land, and got shot at. I thought Ollie Martin would like to know."

"He wouldn't," she said. "Keep off our land and it won't happen."

"It was my back they shot at," Chance said slowly, holding her eyes. "Ollie Martin had better know that I don't like my back shot at. And I hear there's been a lot of it around these parts."

"Tell Ollie that," his daughter said, and, if she felt regret, her face did not show it.

"Too bad I missed him," Chance regretted. "You might tell him, miss, if I don't find him."

"Wait. How do you know it was our men who shot at you?"

"They were on your land."

"That isn't proof."

Chance smiled faintly in the ragged stubble. "Tell Ollie Martin it's proof enough. He won't care . . . but I'd like him to know. I take it no one has ever exactly warned him careful. This is it."

She said again—"Wait!"—as Chance gathered the reins. When he looked at her questioningly, she said: "Who are you?"

"I drifted in, miss. I'll be drifting on again . . . shortly."

"I know that." She stopped, and, strangely, she swallowed. "You're the man Ollie made trouble with . . . just before dark yesterday."

"That's right."

"I heard him telling about it when he got home." She swallowed again. "Where did you get that bent half dollar you were trying to spend? Have you still got it?" She met the cold, probing, nearly hostile edge in his eyes.

"I haven't got it," Chance said. "What difference does it make?"

"Everything. I've got to know."

A galloping rider came toward the house. Chance stepped behind Nelly's horse and slipped the new rifle from the scabbard.

"That's one of our men. You won't need the rifle."

"I see who he is," Chance said. "Same mustache. He's the one who opened up at my back. What's his name?"

"John Burke. He'll not do anything. Not while I'm here with you."

The rider sighted the bay horse and pulled up sharply. Then, apparently satisfied at seeing Lucille Martin, he came on. Chance stepped out into sight when it was too late for the other to ride away.

"Come closer, mister!" Chance called. "Step down and throw your holster on the ground. Then stand away in the open."

Burke was as cold and cool as when he had stood on the cañon bench. He moved, unarmed, into the open, and his eyes roved toward the corrals.

"Been a mistake, hasn't there?" he said. "I didn't know you was a friend of the family."

"You'll learn. Walk back the way you rode in. I'll side you out on foot until a rifle can't reach us." Chance caught the horse's reins and spoke to the girl. "You wouldn't be interested in that half dollar. Ollie Martin said it was junk. Don't forget to tell him I dropped by."

Burke walked stiffly ahead, big, strongly mustached. His dark hat was pulled low over a scowling forehead.

"Your turn now," Burke said over his shoulder. "Going to use it?"

"Wouldn't want to say why you cut down on me?" Chance was leading Nelly's horse, his back shielded from anyone at the house.

Burke answered him sullenly. "I'm not saying anything."

A horse came after them at a run. Chance cocked the handgun he'd bought at Palomas that morning. The rifle was in his other hand, with the reins, as he turned fast.

Lucille Martin caught up with them, topping Burke's horse with the ease of a ranch hand.

"Let him go back," she said to Chance. "You'll be safe while I'm with you."

"Get going," Chance told the man.

Ollie Martin's daughter was pale as they rode on. "You're not a broken drifter like Ollie said you were."

"I've drifted," Chance said dryly.

She sounded stifled. "That half dollar. I've got to know where you got it."

"Why?"

She bit her lip.

Chance watched her emotion without expression.

"Some months ago a man was shot on the Cold Spring Road," she said. "I think no one but the doctor knows that a half dollar in his pocket was hit by the bullet and driven into the wound. The doctor told me. He said he'd sent the half dollar away, as he'd been asked to do before the man died. He wouldn't tell me where he'd sent it."

"Why not?"

She swallowed. "The doctor thought I didn't have a right to know. There can't be two half dollars like the one you brought to Palomas."

"Why didn't you have a right to know?" Chance asked.

He could not see her eyes. They were on the far distance, off side the dusty ranch road. The emotion had left her voice. She was lovely, with the golden hair in silky coils, but she stated a fact that did not seem to trouble her.

"Ollie Martin's daughter didn't deserve to know. It was believed that Ollie wanted the man killed."

"I'm only a stranger," Chance said. "Why should I think differently?"

"No reason," Lucille Martin said. She gave him a look that was like a curtain drawn over pride and anger. She wheeled Burke's horse and lashed it with the rein ends back toward the ranch house.

Twilight was a pale afterglow on the rim of the world when Chance rode to the home corral and dismounted. He waved to Jimmy Dee in the doorway of the bunkhouse, lifted a hand to lanky Ed Peck in the saddle shed. Smoke was coming from the cook house pipe, but the cook was standing in the doorway, watching old Dad Boyle hobble fast out of the ranch house and head toward the corral.

The old man's twisted, shorter left leg and crooked back gave him a crab-like, sidling motion. He looked awkward, but he covered ground swiftly.

The fast fading light did not hide the hostile blaze in the old man's glare, the working of his thin mouth under the drooping, white mustache. He wore two guns, and they were awkward-looking, too, until Dad Boyle's gnarled hands jerked them free, covering Chance.

"Where you been?" the old man asked harshly. His head reared back and up from the crab-like crouch in which he had to stand, but the two cocked guns were steady.

Chance saw Ed Peck moving toward them. Jimmy Dee and three more men were coming watchfully from the bunk-house. All were armed, and threat lay in the twilight.

"I circled out to look around," Chance said. "Anything wrong with that?"

"Where's that hunk of blue-green rock you was baiting the boys with?"

"Hold those guns and I'll show you." Chance held out the bit of rock.

Ed Peck, behind him, suddenly had his gun.

"Fresh chipped," Dad Boyle said harshly. "Just like I thought." He put the rock in his pocket and cursed Chance over the one gun he still held. "Smart trick, gettin' Nelly soft enough to hire you, wasn't it? You low-down crooked snake! I ought t' have the boys drag you off the place with a cow rope! A little lead under your dirty skin'd finish it off right! I knowed when I seen the sorry look of you, there'd be trouble if you hung around."

"What trouble?" Chance asked. "What's happened?"

Ed Peck drawled: "Last Chance, you had a chance, and it's the last you git around here. Jimmy and me got worried about you heading off alone. We turned back and swung over the way you'd gone. Looked for a while like we'd not find you. Jimmy sighted you ridin' west from Teepee Butte. We could just make out Miss Nelly's horse."

"Moving fast toward Ollie Martin's place," said Jimmy Dee.

Dad Boyle choked on the fury that filled him. "Right into Ollie's place to report . . . an' don't lie, you low-down snake! The boys seen you! What you up to? What's Ollie Martin fixin' to try now?"

"Suppose I told you?"

"I wouldn't believe ary damn' word come outta that brush on your face!"

"I'll tell you anyway," Chance said. "Maybe you can read the sign better than I can. There's something up Little Bear Cañon that Ollie Martin's interested in."

"What? Speak out, damn you!" A spasm shook Dad Boyle. "Little Bear Cañon is Nelly's. Ollie Martin wouldn't have that worthless land when he took the Bear Creek Cañon water an' range. He said he didn't want to be a hog, an' he'd just take the Bear Creek side. An' when we wanted to get into Little Bear Cañon, we could ask right-of-way over his land. He knowed there was no other way into Little Bear Cañon that was worth a hoot. I deeded Little Bear Cañon to Nelly, an' now Ollie Martin's after it."

"Seems to be," Chance agreed. "There's gun guards at the mouth of Little Bear Cañon. Sam Wilson got in there, and got away. He was trailed inside your own fence before they killed him. Wasn't that my horse was so fast, they'd have got me." He paused, waiting.

Dad Boyle snarled: "You know too damn' much about it!"

The bent and twisted old man was shaken by another spasm of fury.

Chance had a moment of deep insight, back through the years of which he knew little, back to that long-ago stampede in the pitch-dark night, and the crippled years in a wheel chair that had followed. Years in which Ollie Martin had taken what he wanted. Years in which bitterness and hate had flowered in helplessness. Ollie Martin had always gotten what he wanted.

"You know what Ollie's after?" Chance asked, and he saw that Jimmy Dee and the other men were watching Dad Boyle as well as himself.

"Ollie Martin wants everything! He gits everything," Dad Boyle said harshly. "Always has an' always will, while he can use guns an' tricks and dirty work to git his way!"

"That piece of rock was in Sam Wilson's hand," Chance said. "The men who killed him and stripped his pockets didn't bother with his clenched hand. Sam Wilson knew he was a dead man quick. He grabbed and held one thing that would tell where he'd been after his body was found. I guess he knew all about Miss Nelly's rock you keep on the mantel in the house."

Jimmy Dee said: "I seen Chance fooling around Sam's body just before he showed us that little piece of rock. I see him stoopin' over, pokin' around close to Sam's hand. He said there wasn't any more rock around there looked like it. I said it was like Miss Nelly's rock in the house, that come outta Little Bear Cañon. Last Chance sure did say he might ride near Little Bear Cañon and get him a chunk. Ed and I kinda forgot that when we seen him heading toward Ollie Martin's house."

"Lock him up!" Dad Boyle ordered harshly. "That go-around with the Martin gal is enough fer me. Wouldn't believe anything he said about it. Facts is facts. I ain't got time to take chances. Lock him up in Billy Poor's storeroom. There ain't a window. The lock that'll keep you boys outta Billy's canned peaches will keep him in."

Billy Poor, the cook, was a stringy old-timer like Dad Boyle and with a temper almost as short.

"My storeroom ain't no jail!" the cook protested irritably. "That old fool's askin' me to quit when he gits ideas like this."

"Dad's riled an' worried," said Jimmy Dee. "Better play along with him."

"Twenty-two years I've played along with him an' it ain't no easier now than it was at first. Put him in the storeroom an' git!"

When the door was locked, Chance found a candle stuck on top of a flour barrel. He lighted it and sat heavily on a box of canned milk. Shelves, sacks, boxes were stocked with food. Grub had been served, but the smell of it was still thick and taunting in the cook room and in the storeroom.

Billy Poor was not as cantankerous as he sounded. He unlocked the door. "Step out an' fill up, mister. Even a dog don't sleep hungry around here. Jimmy Dee's sittin' outside the door with a gun in case you hanker to leave quick."

The food was almost as good as Miss Nelly's, in Palomas. Chance said so. Billy Poor scowled at him. "Oughta be better. I taught that gal how to cook when she wore pigtails." Billy Poor slammed some pots and pans around. "She learned faster'n I could teach," he admitted. "Never could get a pie crust like she makes. You got some sense anyways. These hog-trough feeders I got around here don't know good food from slop. I got a extra slab of apple pie left here I guess I can spare."

"Kissin' the cook sure pays better than cussin' him,"

Jimmy Dee chuckled outside the doorway. "Billy, you turn out a handsome meal. A man used to your grub'd starve to death anywheres else. You got anything extra for me in there?"

"Rat poison," said Billy Poor sourly. "I ain't fergot who said my beans was scraped out of a gravel bank."

"I'd 'a' shot that feller myself," Jimmy Dee chortled. "Had my gun out when I remembered it was me said it. Chance, I'll git you some blankets, or an old quilt at least. Anything else you want?"

"Some scissors and a razor," Chance said. "Might as well shave and clean up."

"I'll get my own razor, for the pleasure of seein' what you look like," said Jimmy Dee. "Say some more nice things to our cook in there an' he'll shave you after he runs outta extra pie."

The cook had a piece of broken mirror. He furnished a pan of warm water and a clean towel before he locked Chance back in the storeroom and ordered Jimmy Dee to stay outside.

Chance sat on the box, smoking, after he had shaved and washed. The weariness was deep in his bones again. His head was still sore where Ollie Martin's pistol barrel had split the scalp. He was thoughtful. Once he reached absently to the empty holster at his side, remembered that his gun had been taken from him, and smiled wryly.

After a while he pulled his boots off and soaked blistered feet in the pan of hot water he had asked the cook to leave on the floor, before the door was finally locked for the night. He had walked into Palomas, and the expensive half boots had not been made for walking. The feet in the boots were not used to walking.

He was still soaking his feet by candlelight when he heard the fast drum-pound of running horses come past the house and pull up at the bunkhouse.

He could hear the muted sound of voices. One man was louder than the others, angry, threatening. Billy Poor's voice spoke with bitter caution from outside the storeroom door.

"That's Ollie Martin with some of his gun hands. He wants you, mister. Says he'll drag you down the road for comin' to his place with threats."

"Get me a gun," Chance said. "A good gun, loaded. Unlock the door and Ollie Martin can have me."

III

"CLEAN CHANCE"

"That ain't the way we do things," said Billy Poor. "Ollie Martin'll get you when the rest of us has stopped shootin'. Who does he think he is, ridin' on the place this way, givin' orders?"

Chance listened for a shot. None came. He heard the riders leave. The cook came back in from outside, and spoke through the locked door again.

"Ed Peck out-talked Ollie. Said you must be in town, since you wasn't around the bunkhouse. Ollie said he'd find you." Billy Poor snorted. "Good thing old Boyle wasn't here. He was saying he'd had enough of Ollie Martin. If he hadn't rode to Palomas, the chances are he'd have been out there talkin' with a shotgun. Jack Boyle was a man before he got crippled up. He's still one, inside. When he gets to town, Miss Nelly'll have her job cut out to calm him down."

"Dad Boyle has gone to Palomas?" Chance demanded sharply.

"Yep."

"Martin and his men are heading that way?"

"That's right."

"Unlock the door. Can't you see what's going to happen?"

Billy Poor hesitated, then unlocked the door. He was talking as Chance came out. "I ain't sure what'll happen, but I'm beginning to worry."

"You'd better worry if you think anything of Dad Boyle," Chance rapped at him. "Martin's riled about me. He's worse than riled about Dad Boyle. All he needs is an excuse. If Dad Boyle hits town on the warpath and they meet, Ollie Martin will have his excuse. This time it won't be a cattle stampede. Can you get my gun while I saddle me a horse?"

"Watch me," said Billy Poor in a flat and purposeful voice. "Them fools would 'a' knowed better than to lock you up if they'd seen you with the whiskers off. You look like a man to ride with, mister."

Chance was already going out the door, heading for the saddle shed and the corral. He had a lantern lighted, a rope in his hand, and was over the corral fence when Billy Poor ran to the poles with the guns.

"Take that big blue roan with the white fore hoofs," the cook panted. "He's fresh an' fast and ain't gun-shy."

The other men came tumbling out of the bunkhouse. "We was wondering about Dad Boyle ourselves!" Jimmy Dee called. "Might as well all ride in."

Chance pulled the roan out of the corral, saddled, and was ready to ride before he spoke to the men. They were only five softly cursing figures in the dim lantern light.

"Ride in together looking for trouble, and you'll get it. I'm going first and see what I find. My advice is to scatter and ease into town. Find Dad Boyle, if you can, and keep him quiet. If you think trouble's coming, gather at Miss Nelly's place. But don't act hasty. You're apt to make it worse. The sheriff's a friend of Ollie Martin's."

"You ride on, partner. We'll do what we can," Ed Peck's drawling voice called out of the shadows.

The roan was punished on that fast ride. Now and then Chance pulled up the blowing horse and listened. The mountains in the east were black masses against the bright stars. The gray road dust was a faint ribbon, quickly lost in the ground shadows. Moonlight would have made it easier.

From a hogback rise a few faint lights marked Palomas when Chance heard the steady rhythm of horses ahead. He thought he saw the drift of dust and the darker blot of riders and mounts. It didn't matter. The sound was going away from him, toward town. He jogged behind, and once pulled up abruptly when he sighted a lone rider trailing the others.

He was close when he came, undiscovered, to the first mean shanties of town. Chance turned off there to the right, tied up the roan, and came to the back of Nelly's place.

The Chinaman at the kitchen range gave him an unfriendly look.

"Get Miss Nelly back here," Chance said, unsmiling.

She backed in with an armful of dirty dishes as he finished speaking. Lifted eyebrows were her only signs of surprise.

"Take a seat at the counter, if you're hungry, stranger. We're ready to close, but I guess we can feed you."

Nelly didn't know him, clean-shaven now, with a dark, lean face, thin-lipped, young, with something close to coldness in the chiseled, unsmiling lines of mouth and jaw.

"Is your grandfather here?" Chance asked.

Nelly shook her head. Then suddenly she looked from his boots to the new gun belt and gun.

"So this is what we hired! Last Chance, you do improve after a razor." Her look clouded. "Why do you want him? Has anything more happened?"

"I don't know," Chance said. "Ollie Martin's in town, looking for trouble. Dad Boyle headed this way earlier, set to tangle with Ollie if he had half a chance."

"I've been afraid of it," Nelly said to herself. "All these years it's been coming." She was frightened as she looked at Chance. "Grandfather was in here at noon, to tell me Sam Wilson had been found. He was upset. I talked him into going home. If he's come back, he hasn't let me know." She began to untie her apron as she spoke. Her hands were unsteady.

"You'd better stay here, in case he steps in," Chance suggested.

Nelly said: "If he's in town, I'm going to find him." Her voice did not lift. Only the trembling hands and the quiet purpose in her voice warned him that argument was useless.

"Where can I find the sheriff?" Chance asked.

"He's in the Curly Horn saloon a lot, or out on the street, or in Ollie's Ox-Bow restaurant. He might even be in the jail office, or in his room. He boards with Missus Ryker, back on the next street. Do you know what he looks like?"

"I saw him this morning," Chance said. "Handsome, ain't he? I'll find him." Chance was going, then he turned back, surprising Nelly Boyle's wide-eyed, intent look at his back. "I'd like to carry that half dollar tonight, miss."

"Why?"

"For luck." His smile wiped the chiseled lines into warmth. "Can't ever have too much luck."

Nelly stepped beyond the partition, returned with her handbag, and gave him the coin. "I wish I could add to your luck, Last Chance."

"You did," Chance said, smiling down at her. "I'll tell you

about it later." He was fingering the bent and battered coin as he walked out the back door.

Dad Boyle was not on the street or in the Curly Horn saloon. Ollie Martin was not in the saloon, and Jep Keyes, the sheriff, was not in sight. Burke, the heavy-mustached, powerful gun guard to Little Bear Cañon was drinking near the front of the Curly Horn bar.

Burke glanced indifferently at the tall, clean-shaven stranger who looked in, and turned back to his glass. A moment later when he looked at the door again, frowning, puzzled, the stranger was gone. Burke stood there, toying with his drink, scowling, trying to think.

There was a light on in the jail office at the other end of the street. Through the window Jep Keyes could be seen, leaning easily back in a desk chair and smiling as he talked.

Chance opened the door and entered. Only his eyes warmed with surprise as he saw who the sheriff was talking to.

Lucille Martin looked as cool and pretty as she had that afternoon. Her face was without great warmth, but she had been smiling. The smile lingered as she looked curiously at the intruder.

Jep Keyes, the sheriff, had an easy rangy build and a carefully clipped brown mustache. He dressed fastidiously. A gold watch chain showed in his open coat front as he straightened slowly in the chair. A heavy seal ring was on the hand he placed on the desk. He had a full, handsome mouth and an air of confident swagger, even when he sat. He waited now, eyeing the visitor.

"I stopped in to ask how much murder you stand for in town," Chance said mildly to the sheriff. He saw Lucille Martin start at the sound of his voice and watch intently. He added: "Might as well include all your district in that question."

Jep Keyes was annoyed. "No murder at all. Mind telling me who you are, and what's the idea?"

"I'm in town for a few days," Chance said. "Maybe longer. Dad Boyle headed this way after dark, and Ollie Martin is looking for trouble with him. Dad Boyle won't have a chance if he tangles with Ollie's gun crew, or with Ollie Martin himself. You'll have murder if it isn't stopped."

Jep Keyes leaned back, smiling again. "You are a stranger, mister. Those two men have gotten along for a lot of years without murder."

"Have it your way," Chance said. "I wanted to warn the law for the record. Ollie Martin is looking for me, Sheriff. He left warning at Dad Boyle's place. What do you mean to do about that?"

Red-faced, Jep Keyes snapped: "Nothing. I don't believe you. Martin is our leading businessman and rancher. Sometimes he says things that could be taken wrong. If you're afraid . . . for no good reason . . . you can give up your gun for the night, and I'll lock you in the back. You'll be safe."

"I'll keep the gun and walk the street," Chance said. "But now I've warned you."

Jep Keyes stood up. He was a tall man on his feet, and more than willing to meet the issue. "I don't like the way you're acting, mister. You seem to be looking for trouble. It might be a good idea to lock you up, anyway. Strangers can't come here and make charges and threats against our leading citizens. Not in my office."

Lucille Martin spoke suddenly, standing as she talked. "Don't be a fool, Jep. You've been one too long. Can't you see this man is telling the truth?"

"About your father?" Jep Keyes asked, amazed.

"Don't call him my father. I stopped thinking of him as a father before I was twelve years old. He was only a man who always had his way and made me do exactly as he wanted because he owned me, too."

Jep Keyes looked incredulous. "You've never talked like this before. Why, you heard your father say he'd be glad if we were married."

"Why not, Jep? He knew I didn't love you. If we were married, Ollie would really be able to use you. Everything this man is telling you is the truth."

Chance, watching them, was almost sorry for the handsome Jep Keyes. The man looked like he'd been hit hard, in heart and vanity. He was close to stammering.

"I didn't know you disliked me, Lucille. And you're talking about your own father. This man hasn't any proof."

Lucille was pale, but she had that cool, almost aloof lack of feeling Chance had noticed earlier in the day. "I don't dislike you, Jep. I rather like you. I've never said I wouldn't marry you. Only I've never loved but one man." She looked at Chance as she said it. The lamplight glinted on the silky coils of yellow hair. Her face was composed. Only her eyes had deep, burning emotion. "I loved one man, Jep." Her eyes held Chance's look. "I don't know whether he had anything but the horse he rode into Palomas. But I knew, and he knew, and I was fool enough to tell Ollie." Her head came up. Pride and sadness filled her voice. "My man didn't have anything Ollie could use. He wasn't the kind of man Ollie could order. He was a real man. And when Ollie saw I was going to leave, he warned me it would never happen. So they found my man on the Cold Spring Road, shot by someone who had waited there for him. Ollie was in town, so you knew he couldn't have done it, Jep. But other people guessed who had ordered it. They blamed me, too. Wasn't I Ollie Martin's daughter? Wasn't I selfish and greedy and used to having my own way like Ollie Martin? Wasn't I the kind who wouldn't care whether a man was killed because he loved me? Wasn't I, Jep?"

She was still looking at Chance, and the dam broke suddenly after all the years. Great, tearing, dry sobs shook her as she dropped into the chair.

Jep Keyes was dazed, helpless, not knowing how to meet this.

Chance stepped to the chair. "He was your man, all right. That's something to remember," Chance said quietly. "And all the man you thought he was. We grew up together. I was in Mexico when he wrote me that he'd met a girl he'd never leave. He said there'd be trouble with her father, but that didn't matter."

"No, that didn't matter." Lucille Martin gulped. She had quieted some, listening to each word.

"The half dollar was mailed to me, with a few words telling why," Chance said. "Bob and I earned it together. Our first cash money. We swore we'd always keep it. Sometimes one of us carried it, sometimes the other. But when we met, it had to be shown and passed over to the other to carry."

"No wonder you wouldn't give it up," Lucille choked.

"I started this way as soon as I got it," Chance told her, not caring that Jep Keyes was listening like a stunned and frozen man. "I had to ride out across the border, and, when I hit the first railroad town, I was slugged that night, cleaned of everything I had, and pushed into an empty freight car. When I got off that train, I was miles across the badlands from Palomas, at Mule Streak water tank. I walked it," said Chance, smiling a little. "And that wasn't so good after I got here. I had the old half dollar to get a drink with and decide what to do."

"What were you going to do?" Lucille asked faintly.

"I thought I'd give Bob's half dollar back to the man who bent it up," Chance said. "And maybe tell the girl what Bob thought of her, as his closest friend. She doesn't need that. But if she'd like to have the first money Bob ever earned. . . ."

She took the bullet-twisted bit of silver. "How old was he?" she asked huskily.

"Eight years the week before he earned it," Chance said. "He'd be twenty-six now, as you know. I thought a lot of Bob." Chance turned his head to Jep Keyes. "Bob Cassidy thought she was pretty fine. She must be. Some man will find it out, like Bob did, and have her laughing again, away from Ollie Martin."

Jep Keyes was resting one hand heavily on the desk, looking at the girl as Chance walked out.

A shadowy figure stepped out of the darkness. Chance's gun was halfway out of the holster before he recognized Billy Poor's agitated voice.

"You bringin' the sheriff? I didn't want to bust in there until you was through with him. Seen you through the window while I was huntin' you."

"The sheriff's busy. Has anyone seen Dad Boyle?"

"I might have knowed Keyes'd be busy if Ollie Martin had anything to do with it," Billy Poor said savagely. "Sure. We found Dad Boyle. He's been over to lawyer Blascom's house."

"Get him out of town. Where is he?"

"You get him," Billy Poor groaned. "Dad Boyle has shucked off forty years. He's sittin' at a table in Ollie Martin's Curly Horn bar, with his guns on the table an' a quart of whisky between them. He's tellin' the world what a skunk Ollie Martin is. Miss Nelly walked right in that barroom and tried to get him out. She couldn't, an' she's outside now and don't know what to do."

"Where's Ollie Martin?"

"Over at the Bull Dog bar. Some of his men an' plenty of

his friends are in the Curly Horn. Ain't any doubt Ollie knows what's going on. He'd stay out of it an' let his men take care of Dad Boyle, but I reckon he'll have to cross the street an' settle with Dad this time."

Then they were hurrying through the heavy shadows, with Billy Poor talking fast. "Dad has called Ollie's hand in public before it's played this time. Dad is tellin' the whole town he staked gold claims up Little Bear Cañon twenty year ago, and then kept quiet an' dynamited the ledge down over the vein when he got crippled. He knew Ollie Martin'd be after it, and he wanted it saved for Miss Nelly. That's why he kept Little Bear Cañon when Ollie got Big Bear. That's how come he had the blue rock that Miss Nelly thought was so pretty."

"That wasn't gold ore," Chance said flatly. "Dad Boyle is full of whisky and dreams tonight."

"The blue rock come out of the ledge above," Billy Poor said. "Don't tell me about the gold. I know. It's wire gold, in soft quartz. Rich as any man'll ever find. Maybe there ain't much of it. But what was there at the outcrop is the kind of ore that men start killing over. Old Jack Boyle sat in his wheelchair, an' then hobbled around, knowing what was going to happen if Ollie Martin ever got an idea what was under the old rock slide up Little Bear Cañon."

"Dad Boyle told you all this?" Chance asked doubtfully.

"I was the man who blew up the ledge when Jack Boyle thought he was gonna die," said Billy Poor. "I seen the wire gold and almost went crazy at the sight. Now it's all blowed sky high. Ollie Martin's been doing something up Little Bear Cañon. Maybe he ain't found the vein yet. But he's suspicious. He's got men workin' around there an' keepin' everyone else away. Sam Wilson got up there and came away with a fresh-clipped sliver of that blue rock. There's only one place that blue-green rock outcrops up Little Bear, an' it's in the ledge I blew down over the quartz outcrop. That's proof Martin's working in the right place. Maybe he's found the quartz face and knows the claim still belongs to Jack Boyle and Miss Nelly, only she don't know anything about it. Or didn't until tonight. Mister, ain't it plain why we've been having more trouble around the ranch lately? Jack Boyle's in the Curly Horn with his guns an' whisky bottle . . . Jimmy Dee and Ed Peck, and Poke and Link are back of Dad Boyle's table, waiting for the shootin' to start. They know how much chance they got against that M-O bunch. But they're staying, waiting for Ollie Martin to cross the street and open the party."

"Probably won't be Ollie who opens it," Chance guessed. "Go tell Nelly Boyle to wait in her restaurant."

"Ain't you coming?" Billy Poor asked as Chance stopped.

"Not right now."

The cook stood there, shadowy and peering. His voice shook with quiet scorn. "I thought you'd do to ride with. But you're a stranger, after all, ain't you? Last chance to get out with a safe skin, an' you're takin' it. Sure. I'll tell Miss Nelly. What'd I waste all this time for?"

Billy Poor was muttering wrathfully under his breath as he hurried off.

Chance tested the new gun there on the dark street. It was a little stiff, and the holster was not broken in, but it would have to do. The bone-deep tiredness was with him, and the slash in his scalp still ached, but he was thinking of Bob Cassidy as he walked into the Bull Dog saloon.

Down the street men had been visible in front of the Curly Horn. But inside this saloon there were other men, quite a few. They were at the tables and at the bar. They were laughing, talking. They broke off suddenly when Chance walked in.

All eyes went to him. The feel of trouble was all through

the low-ceilinged room. Talk started up again as they saw the stranger sauntering up to the bar, where Ollie Martin leaned his bulk easily. Martin was talking to the men nearest him. He saw the stranger enter and went on talking, moving only enough to look at one of the tables near the bar.

Burke, the gun guard at Little Bear Cañon, sat there. He did not move when Chance walked in. His smile was a shadow on and off the strongly mustached face when Ollie Martin looked at him.

Chance veered left, sauntered to the table, stopping beside Burke's chair. The man had not expected this. He stiffened and looked up.

"You don't play 'possum well, Burke." Chance chuckled softly. "A shave don't change a man that much. Tell Ollie to come over here."

"The hell I will. What do you want?"

The wall was behind Chance. He looked quickly to right and left and called: "Martin! Join us!"

"Go to the devil!" Ollie Martin snapped. "I'm busy. Don't even know you."

"Last night in the Curly Horn you knew me well enough," Chance said reasonably. "You swung a gun barrel through my hair."

All other talk had stopped. Every man in the place watched them, not sure what was happening, but knowing it was not friendly. Ollie Martin grew red.

"So you're that tramp?" he said roughly. "And now you're talking like a man. Get out."

"No hurry," Chance said. "I'm waiting for word that Dad Boyle has been shot. I'd hate that, Martin. Besides, I'm a friend of Bob Cassidy's, who was shot on the Cold Spring Road. Remember?"

Ollie Martin remembered. So did Burke. The man spread

both his hands on the table, palms down, and began to drum the fingers softly. He was watching Ollie Martin, who stood, glowering and furious.

"Too bad about Bob," Chance drawled softly. "I hear he didn't have a chance, Martin. Dad Boyle deserves a chance. Let's walk across and let him have it. He's crippled . . . but he's sitting in the Curly Horn, waiting. You're the big bull of the pasture, Martin. Walk over and meet Dad Boyle face to face."

"You crazy fool! Burke. . . ."

Burke exploded off the chair in one twisting lunge that brought his grappling arms around Chance at the waist. He was big, powerful, and the surge of his weight carried Chance hard against the wall. Burke's left arm blocked the revolver in the new holster.

They must have worked this way before. Ollie Martin had been set for the fast draw he made. His gun was crashing as Chance freed the blocked revolver with a mighty yank. Burke lunged up, grabbing at it. Ollie Martin's first shot smashed into Burke's back. The second shot hit Chance's shoulder, slamming him once more against the wall. Burke was falling away from him, and Chance dropped with him, crouching. Ollie Martin was big and triumphant at the bar, already grinning as he saw both men dropping in front of his gun. His next shot struck just above Chance's head. Burke rolled limply on the floor sawdust as Chance fired from his crouch, shooting over Burke's body.

Ollie Martin had not expected it. Startled amazement and sudden fear flashed over his satisfaction, and was still there on his wide face when lead tore his throat, and then his chest. He still looked amazed as he fell back against the bar, and tried to hold it, and suddenly dropped heavily.

Chance crouched for a moment, watching him, while the

reek of powder smoke drifted to the ceiling and the quick scramble of the other men in the room stirred slowly at front and back. "Somebody take word to the Curly Horn that there's no pay from Ollie Martin for killing Dad Boyle," Chance said dryly. "Ollie's killed his last man, and shot him in the back, as usual. I'll wait right here for the sheriff."

Jep Keyes was there in less than a minute. He had run from the sheriff's office. He was breathing hard, and he was strangely silent, poker-faced, as he surveyed the dead men, asked brief questions.

"Ollie shot first?" he asked, and there were witnesses enough to tell him so. "Self-defense, I guess," Jep Keyes decided. He drew a long breath. "I'll have to tell his daughter. She'll need someone."

He was looking at Chance, and, when Chance nodded, Jep Keyes turned on his heel like a man who had been undecided, but now knew he was needed.

Chance watched him go and had a quick, clear flash that Bob Cassidy, wherever he was, would be glad of what was written on Jep Keyes's handsome face. Then Chance remembered himself. He spoke to the nearest men. "I'll have to find a doctor before I eat. If someone will tell Miss Nelly to keep her place open for a little, she'll have herself a customer."

They thought that was natural. It seemed natural to Chance as he went to find the doctor.

Last chance, Nelly had told him, last chance to be a man and settle down. She was right, of course, and, like Jep Keyes, Chance knew what he meant to do. He went and set about it.

About the Author

T. T. Flynn was born Thomas Theodore Flynn, Jr., in Indianapolis, Indiana. He was the author of over a hundred Western stories for such leading pulp magazines as Street & Smith's *Western Story Magazine*, Popular Publications' *Dime Western*, and Dell's *Zane Grey's Western Magazine*. He lived much of his life in New Mexico and spent much of his time on the road, exploring the vast terrain of the American West. His descriptions of the land are always detailed, but he used them not only for local color but also to reflect the heightening of emotional distress among the characters within a story. Following the Second World War, Flynn turned his attention to the book-length Western novel and in this form also produced work that has proven imperishable. Five of these novels first appeared as original paperbacks, most notably *The Man from Laramie* (1954) which was also featured as a serial in *The Saturday Evening Post* and subsequently made into a memorable motion picture directed by Anthony Mann and starring James Stewart, and *Two Faces West* (1954) which deals with the problems of identity and reality and served as the basis for a television series. He was highly innovative and inventive and in later novels, such as *Night of the Comanche Moon* (Five Star Westerns, 1995), concentrated on deeper psychological issues as the source for conflict, rather than more elemental motives like greed. Flynn is at his best in stories that combine mystery—not surprisingly, he also wrote detective fiction—with suspense and action in an artful balance. The psychological dimensions of Flynn's Western fiction came increasingly to encompass a confrontation with ethical principles about how one must live, the values that one must hold dear above all else, and his belief that there must be a balance in all things. The cosmic meaning of the mortality of all living creatures had become for him a unifying metaphor for the fragility and dignity of life itself. *Reunion at Cottonwood Station* is his next **Five Star Western.**